THE BAKERY IN BAR HARBOR

Secrets in Maine

BOOK 1

AMY RAFFERTY

Subscribe Here!

Don't miss the
Giveaways, competitions,
and 'off the press' news!

Don't want to miss out on my giveaways, competitions and
'off the press' news?
Subscribe to my email list by going to https://dl.bookfunnel.com/daorxdf4jo
It is FREE!

INTRODUCTION TO THE SECRETS IN MAINE SERIES

SECOND CHANCES DO EXIST ...

'Page-turning with exceptional world-building and realistic characters that are intriguing!
'Amy Rafferty is a brilliant writer and I love all her books. It is impossible to decide which series is her best as they are all fabulous!!!!!!"
'This is going to be an amazing series!'
'Enthralling!!!'

Grab your tissues and go on a journey to **Bar Harbor**, by Amy Rafferty, "The Queen Of Gorgeous Clean Mystery Romance" in the **Secrets In Maine Series.** A heart-warming mystery family saga set in a charming beach resort town in New England.

The Wright siblings are strong and unforgettable, but they all share inner strength, love, quirks, and the ability to support each other through challenges. This family is built on love, laughter, and a unique bond.

Get ready for an exhilarating adventure in The Secrets In Maine series, spanning across seven captivating books. Brace yourself for a cast of vibrant characters who will leave an everlasting impression. Join them as they embark on enchanting journeys, encountering quirky animals, and delving into heartwarming sagas. Experience the thrill of coming-of-age tales and later-in-life romances, with a roller-coaster of emotions that will make you laugh, cry, and yearn for more. This extraordinary series promises an adrenaline-pumping blend of love, tears, and laughter that will keep you on the edge of your seat.

First Love in Bar Harbor (Prequel)
The Bakery in Bar Harbor (Book 1)
The Beach House in Bar Harbor (Book 2)
The Bachelor in Bar Harbor (Book 3)
The Boutique in Bar Harbor (Book 4)
The Sweet Shop in Bar Harbor (Book 5)
The Restaurant in Bar Harbor (Book 6)
The Wedding in Bar Harbor (Book 7)

THE RESIDENTS OF BAR HARBOR

Born to Derek and Clair Wright:

Thorn Wright, age 34
Chase Wright, age 30
Hope Wright, age 26

Born to Stan and Felicia Hall:

Logan Hall, aged 30

CHAPTER ONE

It was a beautiful late spring Sunday morning. Hope was in good spirits as she and her six-year-old daughter, Sydney, pulled up in front of the Hall's house on West Street. The yacht club's fiftieth-anniversary event she'd organized and catered to the previous night had been a huge success. As a result, Hope had been asked to organize and cater two other events. A celebrity winter wedding and the Summer Blast Regatta prize-giving evening.

Hope and Sydney came for lunch with Lavinia and Rodney Hall every Sunday. They had started arriving an hour earlier for dog training lessons for the past eight months. They were barely out of the car when the front door flew open, and Lavinia Hall rushed to meet them.

"Hope, darling, how are you?" Lavinia asked with a smile, giving Hope a hug and a kiss on the cheek.

"I'm good, Lavinia. Just a little tired from the event last night," Hope replied, smiling while Sydney greeted Lavinia with a hug and kiss.

"Hello, Nanna," Sydney grinned and walked around the car with her to where her mother was getting their dog from the backseat.

"Hello, my sweetheart," Lavinia greeted Sydney before commenting to Hope, "I heard that was a smashing success."

"It was, and I got two more events from it." Hope couldn't help the satisfied smile that split her pink bow-shaped lips and lit up her green eyes. "I'm going to be doing the Summer Blast Regatta prize-giving evening, and I've landed my first wedding event."

"That's amazing, Hope." Lavinia was genuinely happy for her. "Rod and I will be at the regatta."

Hope leaned into the car and pulled the leash from between the seats before opening the back door and hooking it onto onto the harness of their one-year-old Cane Corso puppy named Barbie. "I'm so glad I let you talk me into expanding." Barbie jumped out of the car and nearly yanked Hope's arm off as she rushed to greet Lavinia. "I couldn't have done it without you."

"I think we both know that's not true," Lavinia said, taking the leash from Hope to calm the excited dog. "I was merely the sounding board you needed to take the plunge."

"Thank you." Hope breathed in relief, pointing to Barbie when she instantly calmed down and sat patiently beside Lavinia. "I wish I had your magic touch with her."

"I've told you," Lavia stated. "You need to show her who's boss and mean it."

"Mom tries," Sydney told Lavinia. "But Barbie knows Mom is a softie." She giggled at the look Hope gave her.

"You look exhausted, my dear." Lavinia noted the dark circles beneath Hope's eyes. "Why don't Sydney and I work with Barbie today, and you take a break?"

They walked around the side of the sprawling home to the back garden that unfolded its perfectly manicured lawn all the way to the beach. Lavinia led them to the ornate white-washed cast iron garden table and chairs with pretty pink striped cushions beneath a cherry blossom tree.

"I would love to sit and do nothing for an hour." Hope

breathed and looked at Sydney. "But I have to help Sydney with Barbie."

"Mom, I agree with Nan. You should sit and relax today," Sydney told her. "I need to learn how to handle Barbie on my own."

"That's true," Lavinia agreed with Sydney. She glanced toward the back of the house as the Hall's housekeeper walked toward them. "Here comes Cindy now to take your refreshments order."

"Hello, how are you ladies today?" Cindy was in her late forties with slightly graying black hair and big friendly brown eyes. Her round cheeks dimpled into a warm smile.

"Hi Cindy, we're fine. How are you?" Hope replied, sitting down and putting her purse on the table. It always felt like being at a five-star hotel when they visited the Hall's mansion.

"I'm well," Cindy told her. "What can I get you ladies to drink?"

All three ordered iced tea. Cindy left, and Hope sat on one of the garden chairs and plopped her purse beside her. She loved this garden. The grass was always lush green and splashed with color from the large pink and white Cherry blossom trees running down the edge of both sides. As Hope leaned back, watching Lavinia and Sydney prepare for Barbie's training, she realized that Barbie's parents, Quiggly and Maverick, weren't around.

"Where are your dogs?" Hope asked, looking around the garden as Lavinia and Sydney put on their hats.

"I've got them in the side garden," Lavinia told Hope, putting a whistle around her neck. "I'll let them out when we're done." She shook her head and pulled on her gloves. "Barbie just gets too riled up when she sees them."

"I'm going to take Barbie for a walk to the bottom of the garden and back. So long," Sydney told them, leaving before Hope or Lavinia could reply.

They watched Sydney walk off with the oversized puppy

in silence for a few minutes before Lavinia turned to Hope, biting her bottom lip and looking nervous. Hope had seen that look before, which usually meant Lavinia was about to say something that would either upset or shock her.

"While we're alone, I have something to tell you that will make you uneasy," Lavinia lowered her voice. "But it's very exciting news for Rod and me."

Tiny little sparks of shock started to prickle up Hope's spine. "Okay." Her brow furrowed, and her eyes narrowed as she watched and waited for Lavinia's *news*.

Lavinia looked like she was having a war with her emotions. Still, she couldn't contain the excitement that burst into her eyes when she blurted, "Logan is coming home, and it looks like he may be home for good this time." She fixed her gloves. "He has told Rod he wants to help with the grocery and hardware stores."

"Oh!" was the only thing Hope could think of to say as the tiny shocks reverberating through her system turned into high-voltage zaps that shook her core. Her heart had dropped at the mention of Logan's name. "I..." She cleared her throat, which felt like someone was trying to choke her. She quietly drew in a breath and gave Lavinia what she hoped was a confident smile. "I'm very happy for you and Rod. I know how much you've missed your grandson."

Hope's eyes immediately sought out Sydney, who was laughing and prancing about with her dog, blissfully unaware that their whole lives were about to be upended.

"I know this is a big shock." Lavinia smiled encouragingly, following Hope's gaze. "But we all knew it was bound to happen one day."

"I know." Hope nodded and drew in a breath.

"We can discuss what to do about Sydney's schedule, music lessons, and Barbie's training after lunch." Lavinia gave Hope's shoulder an affectionate squeeze. "Let me get Barbie and Sydney to start today's training."

Hope watched Lavinia walk away, calling Sydney and Barbie. Hope's mind spun back to seven years ago as the training began. It was a summer that she would never forget and one where she'd thought all her romantic dreams had come true, only to be smashed apart on the last day. Hope's grandmother always said, *"Feelings and emotions are like glass, and you must handle them carefully. And just like glass, once they are chipped, cracked, or shattered, it's no use trying to repair them. It just leaves ugly scars and too many cracks for everything that was wrong with them before to leak through. It's best to throw the pieces away, and when the time is right, you'll find a new relationship to fill that empty space."*

Her grandmother was right. There was no use trying to hold onto the pieces of her broken heart. Hope had just scooped up all the shattered pieces and locked them away. Luckily it was not long until she'd found another deeper and stronger love. The love of a child. Hope had poured all her time and emotions into Sydney, her baby girl. She smiled as she watched her daughter and Lavinia train Barbie, who was almost as big as Sydney. She was Hope's world. A world that Hope knew was on a collision course with destiny that was about to derail her life and tip out all her neatly concealed secrets. The ones that Hope knew would one day come back to haunt her.

There were only six people who knew who Sydney's father was. Those six people were Clair, Hope's mother, her oldest brother Thorn, her cousin Marli, Sydney's pediatrician Doctor Meldan, Lavinia, and her husband, Rodney. At least four of those people had warned her about keeping the secret over the past six years. Hope could hear her mother's voice in her head telling her it was better to get ahead of the truth before it got ahead of her because it was one race Hope didn't want to lose. Clair Wright was worried about how much worse the fallout from the truth coming out on its own would be rather than coming from

Hope. As if she didn't know that already. Hope hated keeping secrets.

Her eyes fell on Sydney, and her heart twinged. Hope especially hated keeping secrets from her daughter. Hope had rationalized that she'd tell Sydney who he was when she asked about him; however, her daughter had never asked. But Hope feared that was about to change as she knew it would one day. She just wasn't ready for one day to have arrived. Hope took a breath and pinched the bridge of her nose, nearly dying of fright when a deep voice came up behind her.

"I can tell that Lavinia has dropped the bombshell on you about Logan." Rodney Hall's kind blue eyes met hers, and he gave her a warm smile.

"Hi, Rod," Hope greeted him as he sat beside her, facing the garden to watch Barbie being trained.

"Hello, my dear." Rod sat back and linked his hands in front of him, turning his attention to Sydney. "You've raised a fine young lady there," he complimented Hope. "Lavinia and I have been so grateful to you for letting us be a part of that."

Hope turned to watch Sydney and Lavinia when she heard her daughter laughing as Barbie jumped for the ball Lavinia threw at her and landed in the fountain. A smile split Hope's lips when the laughter turned to screams as Barbie jumped out of the water and shook herself next to Sydney and Lavinia.

"She loves you and Lavinia so much," Hope said, turning to Rodney as Cindy walked over to them with the iced tea. Hope and Rod thanked her and waited for her to walk away. "You have both helped us so much over these past six years, and I don't know what I would've done without you."

"Oh, my dear," Rod said, leaning in to pour iced tea into two glasses. "You and Syd came into our lives when we needed the two of you the most." He sat back and took a sip of his tea. "I know we tried to be supportive, and we are so proud of him. But when Logan left to join the Navy Seals...."

His voice grew hoarse with emotion. "You gave us something else to focus on."

Before they could continue the conversation, Lavinia and Sydney let Barbie loose and came to join them.

"Pops!" Sydney's eyes lit up when she saw Rod, and she threw her arms around his neck to hug him and kiss him hello.

"Hey, ladybug." Rod grinned, tickling her and making her giggle. "I see you're getting quite the pro at handling your beast."

"Barbie's not a beast, Pops," Sydney defended her dog. "She's just big and clumsy."

"Tell that to poor Pete, the postman," Rod reminded her. "Barbie nearly knocked him flying the other day."

"Well, the man shouldn't have been standing blocking our doorway trying to chat up Cindy," Lavinia pointed out. She poured Sydney and herself some iced tea before taking a seat and changing the subject. "We have your favorite for lunch today, Hope."

"Ah!" Hope nodded, and her eyes narrowed suspiciously. "Which of my favorite meals?" She asked to gauge what other surprises or awful news Lavinia was about to drop on her.

"Roast lamb with those mini roast potatoes and pumpkin," Lavinia told her, sitting back and sipping her tea. "After lunch, Cindy will take Sydney to watch that new Disney movie on the T.V. so we can talk about the new arrangements."

"Do you mind if I let Quigley and Maverick out to come to play with Barbie and me?" Sydney asked Hope and Lavinia.

"If your mother doesn't mind, honey," Lavinia smiled at her. "I'm sure Quigley and Maverick are dying to see you both."

"Of course, honey," Hope said. "Just be careful, okay?"

"Sure," Sydney promised, downing her iced tea before calling Barbie and taking off for the side garden.

As soon as Sydney was out of earshot, Hope turned to look at Lavinia, "Okay, what else do you have to tell me?"

"Why would you think we had something else to tell you?" Lavinia asked innocently.

"Because you made all my favorite foods," Hope answered. "If you'd had the dishes made because of the news about Logan, you would've led with that. But you waited until after you'd told me that news, which means something else is happening" She poured another glass of iced tea. "I know it is something big because you don't like croquette potatoes."

"Fine." Lavinia sighed and looked at Rod, who Hope noticed was frowning at her as if he was confused. "Logan isn't the only one who's coming home." She bit her bottom lip. "Stan and Felicia are arriving a week after Logan."

"Oh!" Hope raised her eyebrows. "They've been back here since Sydney was born." Her brows creased. "Why is this time different?"

"Because they're bringing the celebrity entourage with them this time." Lavinia moved uncomfortably in her seat. "Including a few nosey reporters."

Hope's heart jolted at the word reporters.

"Lavinia...." Rod leaned forward. "Why is this the first time I've heard about Stan coming home?"

Felicia and Stan Hall were Logan's parents, and Stan was Lavinia and Rod's only son. They were also extremely well-known celebrities which made Hope nervous because the last thing she wanted was for her association with the Halls to be splashed in all the tabloids. It would be good for her bakery and catering business. Still, it would *not* be good for her family, especially Sydney.

Later that afternoon, as Hope pulled into her driveway, she could've sworn she saw someone watching her from across the street in a blue sedan. After getting Sydney and Barbie inside, Hope went to the living room window and saw that the car was still there. While Sydney bathed, Hope took

Barbie for a quick walk and noticed the car was still parked there. She also saw that the man in the car had a camera.

An instant spark of anger flamed Hope's belly. She'd protected her daughter for the past six years from nosey reporters who had been at her bedside the day she'd given birth. All because she'd been taken to the hospital by Lavinia Hall, who stayed with her during the birth. Over the past six years, Hope had been stopped by the odd reporter. They always asked about her association with the Halls, having noticed how often Hope and Sydney visited them.

But Lavinia had told Hope what to say to them, and her answer was always the same. Sydney was a gifted musician, and Rod was helping to hone her skills. Because Lavinia had helped Hope on the day she'd had Sydney, they had become close. Lavinia and Rod were Sydney's honorary grandparents. For a month, the press had swarmed around her. Lavinia and Rod had given an interview explaining their relationship with Hope and Sydney. Eventually, the interest in Sydney and Hope died down.

A week before Hope had known Logan was coming home to Bar Harbor, she was sure someone was following her. But a few days later, she decided she was just being paranoid. Tonight she knew she was *not* being paranoid. The man in a car was watching her. Hope walked down the street, pretending not to notice the car. When she turned to walk back toward the bakery, she was going to try to get a sneaky picture of the car's license plate, but it was gone.

Later that night, before Hope crawled into bed, she checked the window, but the car was nowhere in sight. As she climbed into bed and drifted to sleep, her mind was filled with images of the best and worst ten days of her life as Logan's face filled her dreams.

CHAPTER TWO

Logan stared at the ocean off the balcony of his parent's Malibu beachfront house. The California sun beat down on him as he adjusted his baseball cap and shades. It was hot outside, but the heat couldn't compare to his unease. His parents had been fussing over him since he'd been injured on his last mission as a Navy Seal ten months ago. They wanted him to stay in California, to recover fully and enjoy the life of a hero. They wanted him to bask in the limelight, to be a celebrity like they were.

But Logan couldn't stay here. He needed to go home to Bar Harbor, where he'd grown up and where his heart still belonged. He couldn't let his parents dictate his life any longer. The constant flow of people in and out of their lives. The parties they'd tried to convince him to attend with them, and then there was all the matchmaking. Just because his parents were married before they were thirty didn't mean Logan wanted to follow in their footsteps. His mother had been upset with him when he'd broken off his engagement to his longtime girlfriend, Melissa Shaw, a month before he'd been injured.

Logan had upset his mother once again when he'd told her

he wanted to go home to Bar Harbor, and this time he was thinking of settling there. Felicia Burns was a top-class actress, but even she couldn't fake the hurt that resonated in her eyes when he'd told her his plans. Logan knew his parents had secretly hoped he would come to his senses and take over the family's movie and record studio.

But it was not the life for him, and it was just one of the reasons he'd broken off from Melissa and turned down all the other stars his mother had paraded in front of him. And to make it up to her, Logan had agreed to do something he had managed to do so well so far. Have an interview with someone from a magazine and tell the story of Logan Hall. The elusive and heroic son of the famous Stan Hall and Felicia Burns and ex-fiance of America's sweetheart, Melissa Shaw. He suppressed a shudder as the reporter's voice cut through his musing.

"Your mother said you were a very private person." Annabell Preston watched him intently. She was a reporter for Starz Magazine, one of the most prominent magazines in the country. "She thought you would feel more comfortable talking to me. Someone from Bar Harbor."

"My mother was wrong," Logan retorted with narrowed eyes. "I'm not comfortable talking to any reporter. No matter where they come from or whether their parents are good friends with mine." He eyed her coolly. "Especially one with your ruthless reputation for extracting the truth from your subjects."

"Your mother contacted me, Logan," Annabell reminded him in no uncertain terms. "She flew me here from Boston. I didn't ask for this assignment." Her eyes narrowed. "But after I thought about it, I realized that it would be better for me to do a piece on you rather than some rag who'd twist your words so they could sell more dirt."

"I'm sorry, Annabell," Logan apologized for being rude.

"Unlike my parents, I don't want my story splashed over magazine pages for the entire country to read."

"I understand." Annabell gave him a tight smile. "You grew up with a famous family but always tried your best to keep out of their spotlight." She fiddled with her mini recorder. "I always admired that about you."

"Thank you," Logan said. "My grandparents left showbiz behind when my father was born. They didn't want him to always have a spotlight illuminating him while he was growing up." He shifted in his deck chair as his leg and hip ached. "They wanted my father to have as normal a childhood as possible."

"That's why you grew up in Bar Harbor with your grandparents," Annabell guessed. "So you also got to have a normal childhood."

"Yes," Logan confirmed. "At first, my mother wanted to flaunt me to the world, but my father wouldn't let her."

"How did your mother react to that?" Annabell raised an eyebrow knowingly. "She is a bit of an exhibitionist when it comes to showing off her life."

"I wish I could jump to her defense here and say I disagree." Logan laughed. "But I can't deny the truth of that." He shook his head. "My mother didn't come from a show business background, and my father did," he explained. "My father stepped into the life my grandparents had already set the stage for. My mother had to fight her way into it."

"Wasn't your mother a child star like your ex-fiancee, Melissa?" Annabell asked.

"She was." Logan nodded. "My mother made her father take her to an audition for the sitcom, *The Trouble with Daisy*, when she was ten."

"And she got the part of Daisy Marigold in that sitcom," Annabell remembered. "I used to love watching the reruns of that show when I was a kid."

"Yes, as you know, my mother played Daisy Marigold from

age ten and was with the show for twenty years before it was finally canceled."

"Why did they cancel it?" Annabell frowned. "If I remember, the show had a high rating throughout its history." She tapped her pen against her lip. "I read that it was one of the television networks' most successful shows ever."

"My mother loves to tell everyone that." Logan sighed. "And I believe it was one of the highest-rated shows on the network up until the show's original producer, Gerald Stern, died in a car accident." He scratched the back of his neck. "My mother said the show seemed to have lost its spark like the heart of it died with Gerald."

"I looked up some of the reports on the accident," Annabell told him. "The brakes on Gerald's car failed as he was going around a steep curve on a mountain pass."

"I don't know many details about the accident as I was eleven then, but I remember it was horrific." Logan shuddered, remembering it. "My mother was in shock for days after hearing about it and seeing pictures of the car wreckage."

"There was a lot of speculation over how the accident mimicked the one Gerald had written into *The Trouble with Daisy*." Her eyes narrowed thoughtfully. "Right down to the pass where it happened."

"I believe so." Logan's eyes narrowed suspiciously. "Although I'm not sure what relevance a nineteen-year-old accident has to do with this interview?"

"Oh, this isn't part of the interview. It's just me getting to know you and your family a little better." She gave him a bright smile.

"Annabell, your father and mine went to school together and were best friends," Logan reminded her. "Not to mention, your mother was my mother's best and only friend. I'm sure you know my family very well."

He frowned when he saw something flash in her eyes at

the mention of her mother, but it was gone too fast for him to decipher it.

"I know them in a social setting or through my family," Annabell told him. "I don't know them like I need to get into your head and how you feel about them." She laughed. "And because I loved that show and thought that Gerald Stern was a genius and your mom was the best actress ever." She flipped her pen between her fingers. "Each season, I couldn't wait to find out what new character would be joining the show, and it was usually always an unknown young rising star." As she reminisced, she looked at Logan with excitement sparkling in her hazel eyes. "It really earned its nickname of being the show that was the showcase for hot new talent."

"Introducing new young stars each season was my mother's idea," Logan said. "The show had given her a foot in the door to stardom and launched her career. My mother wanted to give kids starting out a chance as she knew how hard it was."

"Newcomers to showbiz, like Melissa Shaw," Annabell stated cleverly, bringing the conversation back to Melissa.

"I guess." Logan shrugged, and his eyes narrowed as he crafted his answer carefully, knowing it was some sort of a trap.

"Wasn't *The Trouble with Daisy* the show that launched Melissa's career?" Annabell persisted with her line of questioning.

Annabell truly was the crafty reporter she had the reputation of being.

She should've been an interrogator, Logan thought. "Maybe. But I'm sure, as Melissa's father is a top Hollywood executive, she would've made it even if she didn't get the part of Chelsea Cohen on the show."

"Wasn't it your mother who insisted on having a part for Melissa written into the show?" Annabell looked at him questioningly.

"I believe so," Logan once again gave a vague answer, trying to figure out where Annabell was going with her line of questioning.

"The new parts for the season were already filled, but your mother insisted that Gerald get Melissa onto the show," Annabell stated. "That was after Melissa had already auditioned for the part of Daisy's long-lost daughter but lost the part to Hazel Ash."

"As far as I know, my mother was impressed with Melissa's audition. She wanted her in the show," Logan told Annabell, getting irritated with her line of questioning. "My mother came up with the idea in the script to make Melissa the ten-year-old daughter of her best friend."

"The daughter who she's the guardian of comes to live with Daisy when her parents are killed in a car crash where their brakes failed, and they went over a cliff on a mountain pass." Annabell tilted her head as she looked at him, squinting. "For a year, there were rumors that your mother and Melissa's father fought for her to have a bigger role in the sitcom."

"I don't know anything about that," Logan lied.

"Then, on the first anniversary of Melissa starting on the show, Gerald dies in almost the exact same way that Melissa's television parents did." Annabell pointed out. "That's quite a coincidence, isn't it?"

"What are you getting at?" Logan looked at her suspiciously. "Is this about the rumors that Gerald's family started about Melissa's family or my mother having something to do with that accident?"

"Oh, gosh, no," Annabell said innocently, but there was a look in her eyes he didn't trust. "Your mother and the Shaws were exonerated of the accusations that the Stern family brought against them."

"Annabell, what has all this got to do with my interview?" Logan asked her, not able to mask the annoyance in his voice.

Nor did he think for a second that she believed what she'd just said.

"Melissa once mentioned that you had met when you were ten. She also implied the two of you had always been close," Annabell quoted from Melissa's interview about their relationship.

"That's correct." Logan nodded. "We did meet when we were ten."

"Only it wasn't you and Melissa that was close, was it?" Annabell reached next to the chair and pulled a copy of an old photo from her briefcase, placing it on the table between them and pushing it toward him. "But you and Hazel Ash were."

His heart lurched when he saw the picture of eleven-year-old him on his bicycle and Hazel perched on his handlebars.

"Where did you get this?" He glared at her.

"You know I can't reveal my sources," Annabell told him. "But you can answer my question."

"Of course, I was friends with Hazel as well," Logan ran his hand over the photo before pushing it back to Annabell. "I knew most of my mother's co-workers."

"But you were only ever really in love with one of them when you were sixteen, though," Annabell pulled another old photo from her case and pushed it toward him. "And it wasn't Melissa Shaw."

Logan's heart lurched, and he swallowed as his throat suddenly went dry when he saw the picture Annabell had displayed. He was standing next to Melissa on the red carpet at the premiere of *Sky Twins*. Melissa's first starring role alongside Logan's mother and Hazel, who was standing next to dashing Chase, who looked like the cat that got all the cream. It was the only time he'd ever felt jealous of his best friend or wanted to punch him. Only two females had ever made his heart lurch or stomach knot with emotion, and right now, he was staring at the first woman to have made him feel that way.

Hazel Ash. She was gorgeous, with her exotic looks, silky straight dark hair which always shone and glinted with deep fiery red tints when the light hit it. Hazel's creamy smooth skin highlighted her delicate bone structure and perfectly sculpted features. She always had a quick smile that warmed her hazel eyes and sparkled with her kind nature.

"What has this to do with my choice to join the military instead of becoming a star or taking over the family movie and record studio?" Logan asked her, getting annoyed with her questions about his past. "I thought this interview was supposed to be about me not wanting to go into show biz, joining the military, and what I would do with my life now that I've retired."

"Everything!" Annabell assured him. "And as I said before, the interview hasn't formally started yet." She raised her eyebrows. "I'm merely warming up. I'm learning a bit about your past relationships. That way, I get a feel for what's happening in your life now."

"I'd rather speak about what's going on in my life now," Logan told her. "Because I don't see how digging up my past has anything to do with what's going on in my life right now."

He glanced at the picture of Hazel and could remember the night the photo had been taken as if it was yesterday. Logan had just celebrated his sixteenth birthday. Hazel had attended the party, and they had kissed for the first time. She'd followed him out to the pool area of his grandparent's house in Bar Harbor, where he'd stormed out too. Logan had been so furious with his mother, who'd once again turned one of his birthday parties into an advert for her upcoming movie premieres. Hazel had felt awful because she and Melissa, who was also at his party, were co-stars in the movie with his mother. She had felt like she was partly to blame for ruining his birthday, and they had spoken outside for ages before they had shared one magical kiss.

That movie had been Melissa's first movie. The one that had moved her up the ranks to America's sweetheart. Melissa had played the role of the younger of the two non-identical twin sisters. It was a sci-fi movie set two hundred years into the future. Her character was sweet, kind, caring, and self-sacrificing. It had become the character that Melissa's super-star image had been molded around. Hazel had played the cold, hard, get-it-done-whatever-it-took sister, and was the last movie she starred in. Logan had thought that they had cast them in the wrong roles, but Hazel had once again proven what a terrific actress she was when she'd aced the part. Logan had spent days after his birthday trying to pluck up the courage to call Hazel and ask her if he could escort her to it. He'd even written a song for her, not that he'd ever told anyone about it, nor would he admit it. Music had always secretly been his outlet for his emotions.

Chase and Rose, his best friends, were the only two people to know how much he loved to create music. Thank goodness he'd never told them about his feelings for Hazel because he'd have had to face more than a broken heart. Right before Logan had finally plucked up the courage to call Hazel, his mother had found him. She demanded that he take Melissa to the premiere. He'd argued that he didn't want to take Melissa and told her he was about to call Hazel. She'd told him in no uncertain terms that Hazel had asked Chase to escort her, and it was Chase Hazel was trying to get the attention of at Logan's birthday party.

Logan had been devastated and agreed to go with Melissa, which turned into their first date and the turning point where he decided show business was not for him. He'd locked away his songbook and never touched a musical instrument again. His parents had been beside themselves when Logan decided he wanted to join the Navy. It was also the year he realized how manipulative his mother could be when she pushed Logan and Melissa together. She did that by making a deal with Logan, and as long as his mother agreed to let him live his life how he wanted to, he went along with her plan. Logan had played the part of the hero to Melissa's princess. Logan had been so busy with his Navy career and wanting to get into the Navy Seals program that he'd just let his supposed relationship with Melissa ride.

But seven years ago, he'd gotten into the training program, and his life had changed. He knew it was time to take control, end things with Melissa, and step out of the sidelines of Melissa's and his parents' spotlight once and for all. He had four weeks' leave due to him, which he took before starting Seal training. Logan made plans to meet up with his friends in Bar Harbor, and he wasn't expecting to find the second but greatest love of his life. But once again, right before Logan was going to take things to the next level with someone he'd given his heart to, it had been ripped out of his chest and stomped on.

So Logan agreed when his mother asked him to take Melissa back after she was jilted by her new rockstar fiance. Up until eleven months ago, he'd let the relationship continue. He wasn't a fool, Logan knew there was no way Melissa had remained faithful to him over the years, but he couldn't blame her for that. Other than being engaged for publicity's sake, there was no way Logan would take the relationship further. He may be a bit jaded about love after his experience with it. However, he still knew that being in a relationship without it was like staring at a whitewashed wall for the rest of his life.

"Logan?" Annabell's voice broke through his thoughts. "Have you heard a word I said?"

"I'm sorry, I was just thinking how much simpler life was when I was eleven," Logan lied.

"Why didn't you ever pursue a relationship with Hazel?" Annabell asked him.

"Hazel had aspirations to become a supermodel and didn't want any commitments or romantic attachments to get in her way." Logan shrugged. "I found I was more suited to Melissa." He sighed. "Now, can we please move forward from my sixteen-year-old self?"

"Sure." Something sparked in Annabell's eyes, making him feel like he was about to regret what he'd just said. "How did you feel when Chase and Hazel started dating five years ago?"

"What?" Logan spluttered. "I...." He shook his head, wondering if something was wrong with his memory from the accident. He'd forgotten Chase telling him about Hazel.

"Oh!" Annabell's eyes widened in fake surprise. "You didn't know?"

"Why do I get the feeling you knew I didn't know, and you're leading up to something bigger?" Logan's eyes narrowed suspiciously.

Pinpricks started to zip up his spine, and alarm bells began to ring in his ears at the look that crossed her face before she dropped her bomb on him. He watched her casually lean over to her briefcase and pull another picture out of it. This one she held to her chest.

"I thought you and your two best friends had no secrets from each other?" Annabell tilted her head and looked at him curiously.

"Why do I feel this is a trap?" Logan's unease grew as she held onto the photo for a little longer. He felt like he was on one of those shows where they paused for a few seconds before letting you know if you won a prize.

"Because it's not only Rose and Chase keeping secrets." Annabell's eyebrows were raised as she put a picture in front of him that made his blood run cold, and his heart stopped beating for a few seconds. "But I do wonder whose secret will feel like the worst betrayal of friendship trust, though?"

She tapped the picture that had somehow been taken summer, seven years ago, of him and Hope Wright kissing beneath the boardwalk in Bar Harbor.

"Where did you get this?" Logan picked up the picture.

"You know I can't tell you that," Annabell told him. "And maybe you shouldn't be as worried about where I got it from but rather how or why it was taken in the first place."

She pulled a document from her bag and placed it face down on the table between them.

Logan's eyes narrowed, "That was going to be my next question."

"I can't answer the why. But I have my suspicions, and I do know the who, but once again...." Annabell trailed off.

"You can't reveal your sources," Logan hissed, getting frustrated.

"I have to go to the bathroom," Annabell tapped the upside-down document. "Please don't go through my stuff while I'm gone."

To his surprise, she winked at him, pushed herself out of the chair, and left Logan alone with the document and her briefcase. A slow smile split his lips as he realized what she'd meant. Logan looked toward the door as Annabell disappeared around a corner in the house before picking up the document and froze.

Crow Private Security had been hired to follow Logan and document who he was with and where he went. Who had hired them and why was it redacted? Logan looked inside the house for signs of Annabell and saw the coast was still clear. He glanced at her chair to see she'd moved her briefcase to the side where he could reach over and get it. Logan pulled the case to him and shook his head.

"You really are crafty, Annabell." Logan whistled under his breath as he pulled out a folder labeled Logan Hall.

He opened it only to find more pictures from the summer

seven years ago. Logan's heart thudded when she saw the pictures of him and Hope.

"What the heck?" Logan's eyes widened when he put the pictures aside to look at the other, and he saw that he wasn't the only one the company had been following that year. There were pictures of his friends and their families, especially of Hope. "What on earth?"

CHAPTER THREE

Hope's dreams had been plagued with images of Logan and nightmares of Sydney disappearing. She had hardly gotten any sleep over the past two nights since Lavinia had told her Logan was coming home for good. Hope had also been walking around with a headache from all the stress and worry about her secret. Especially knowing his parents were also coming back to town the week after Logan arrived.

"Mommy," Sydney's voice echoed down the hallway of their apartment above her bakery and coffee shop, the Cookie Dough Bakery. "I can't find my sneakers."

Hope rubbed her aching temples as she crawled to look beneath her bed for her own sneakers, which were both missing. She sat back on her haunches and shook her head. This could only be the work of Barbie. Hope sighed and stood up.

"I think Barbie took our sneakers again," Hope told her daughter, who was now standing in the doorway of Hope's room.

"I'll go check her bed." Sydney's long dark brown hair was scooped back into a ponytail and swished as she spun around, taking off to check Barbie's bed for their shoes. She called over her shoulder, "I think she hides them beneath the cushion."

"As long as she hasn't started chewing on them," Hope muttered, walking after Sydney.

Hope walked into the living room where Barbie usually slept when she didn't sneak into Sydney's room at night. Barbie was hopping around excitedly as Sydney pulled the cushion off Barbie's doggie bed.

"Good grief!" Hope stared in amazement at everything Barbie had stashed in her bed.

"There's my storybook," Sydney said, picking up the latest book Clair had written. Sydney always got a signed advanced copy of her books. "And my belt, my raggedy Anne doll." She shook her head at her dog. "Barbie, you can't go stealing people's stuff."

"Are our shoes there?" Hope walked into the living room and dropped to her knees next to her daughter.

"No," Sydney said, shaking her head as she gathered everything Barbie had stolen from her room. "I hope she didn't bury them in the back garden again."

"Put your sandals on," Hope said, looking at the time on her wristwatch. "We don't have time to go on a treasure hunt for our shoes if Barbie has buried them."

"And they'll need a wash before we can wear them," Sydney pointed out. "I can wear my sandals today. Alexa says it's going to be hot."

"You know that Alexa isn't always right," Hope warned. "But if you're sure you're okay with wearing your sandals, that will save us a lot of time."

"Okay, Mommy," Sydney dashed off to get her sandals with Barbie close behind her.

Hope looked at her bare feet with her pink-painted toes. "I guess I'd better put some sandals on as well."

She returned to her bedroom and pulled on her sandals when her phone rang. It was her oldest brother, Thorn.

"Hi," Hope answered her phone.

"Hey, little sister," Thorn greeted her. "How are you today?"

"Other than having to buy a shovel to find where Barbie's buried our sneakers, I'm fine," Hope said, her eyes narrowing suspiciously. "Why?"

"Oh no, did she bury your shoes again?" Thorn said evasively. "You can borrow my shovel. Just swing past my house and pick it up. You know where it is in the barn."

"If I go that way, I will. Thank you," Hope said. "So, what's up?" She glanced at the clock over her bedroom door. "Aren't you usually doing some animal surgery this time in the morning?"

Thorn was now the local vet in Bar Harbor.

"No, but I do have to go help with some sick cattle about an hour out of town today," Thorn told her.

"Oh, do you want me to pick up Aaron and Tate after school?" Hope asked.

"Oh, no, Mom's going to do that for me if I'm not back in time to pick them up," Thorn said. "But I do have another *huge* favor to ask of you, and I know you're going to freak out, but I will owe you big time for doing it."

"Please tell me you don't want me to go with you to help with the sick cattle." Hope shuddered, remembering the few times she'd gone to help him with ranch emergencies. "You know I'm not good with blood or livestock."

"I think you're just fine with them," Thorn stated. "But no, it's not that."

"Okay...." Hope frowned, wondering what else he could want her help with that would freak her out.

"Lavinia and Rod are in Bangor for Rod's checkup with the cardiologist," Thorn reminded her, and an uneasy feeling started to creep into her stomach. "They asked me if I could pick up Logan from the ferry this morning, and I was going to, but now I can't."

"Uh-huh!" Hope said, her heart pounding in her chest as her mind spun.

"Mom's car is in the shop until mid-day, or I'd ask her to do it," Thorn's voice dropped. "I know it's a big ask, but please, can you get him?"

"Can't he get a cab?" Hope asked. "We do have Uber now."

"Hope you don't even have to speak to him," Thorn said. "Just dump him in the car and take him home."

"Fine!" Hope hissed. "But you're right. You owe me big for this."

"I do!" Thorn agreed. "Thanks, little sister. Now I have to go if I'm going to get the kids to school on time. Love you."

"I love you, too," Hope said before hanging up.

Her hand shook as she sat on her bed, staring at her phone, wondering why she hadn't come up with some excuse for not picking up Logan. It wasn't more than a few minutes ago Hope had decided to let fate decide how to play the Logan situation. And it seemed that fate was more than happy to oblige by throwing them together the moment he set foot back on Bar Harbor.

"So much for avoiding Logan for as long as I could!" Hope muttered as she grabbed her keys and purse.

"What did you say, Mommy?" Sydney smiled up at Hope as they met in the hallway.

"Oh, nothing, sweetheart," Hope smiled back at her. "Have you got everything?"

"Yup." Sydney nodded, grabbing the stair rails as Barbie pushed past them to pound down the stairs. "I'll let Barbie into the back garden and check the gate while you get the car."

"Great thinking, kid," Hope said before walking to the side door while Sydney went through the back room on the ground floor that led to their small rear garden. "Ensure the gate is secure so Barbie doesn't get into the park again."

"Will do!" Sydney shouted as Hope heard the back door opening.

Their garden backed onto a large park which backed onto a wood and a lake. There was also a large pond in the middle of the neat park, usually filled with beautiful water birds during the spring and summer. As it was the end of spring, the pond was filling up, and the one thing Lavinia had yet to teach Barbie was not to chase birds. While they allowed animals in the park, they had to be strictly supervised and kept away from wildlife. Hope had already gotten a few warnings from a park caretaker about Barbie, who kept threatening that the next time Hope would be fined. It had cost her a fortune in pastries as an apology to the caretaker and his wife.

Hope walked to her garage, opened it, and went to pull her car out when Sydney stepped through the side door and pulled it closed.

"Barbie's all secure in the back garden," Sydney told Hope as she slid into the back seat and buckled up. "I made sure she had food and water, and the shed is open for her to go into if she wants to sleep."

"Did you check her bed in the shed for our sneakers?" Hope asked as it dawned on her that there was another bed Barbie loved to hide things.

"Oh, no, I didn't," Sydney said apologetically. "I'll check when I get home after school."

"It's okay, honey," Hope said, backing out of the driveway. "I'll check after I've dropped you off and run an errand for Uncle Thorn."

"Does he have a stray kitten that needs a home?" Sydney looked at Hope wide-eyed with excitement.

"No," Hope emphasized the word. "I think we have quite enough animals with Barbie and Morris."

"Did Uncle Thorn say when Morris would be able to

come home?" Sydney asked as soon as Hope mentioned their four-year-old blue-point Siamese cat.

Morris had surgery for an obstruction in his stomach which turned out to be one of Sydney's marbles he'd swallowed.

"I still don't understand why that cat would've swallowed one of your marbles," Hope shook her head, remembering how amazed she'd been when Thorn had told her what he'd found in Morris's bowel.

"It was my fault, Mommy," Sydney's eyes darkened sadly. "I was the one that left them lying on the ground."

"No, honey, it wasn't your fault," Hope looked at her daughter in the mirror. "You know Morris, he's always eating the craziest things."

"Well, I've locked the marbles away for good," Sydney assured her. "I don't want Morris or Barbie eating them ever again."

"You don't have to stop playing with your marbles," Hope told her as she pulled into the drop-off zone of the elementary school. "Just remember to pack them away when you're done."

"Sure," Sydney said, unbuckling the seatbelt and scooching forward to kiss Hope goodbye.

"I'll pick you up after swimming," Hope called through the window as Sydney climbed out of the car and closed the door.

"Okay, Mom," Sydney waved.

"I love you," Hope's voice caught in her throat. She had no idea why she still teared up whenever she dropped her daughter off at school.

"Love you too, Mommy," Sydney said, turning and running off to meet her best friend, who was waiting for her through the entrance gate.

Hope pulled out of the drop-off area and glanced at the clock on her dashboard. She didn't have long to get to the ferry, which would be arriving any minute if it hadn't already. Hope drew a deep breath steadying her beating heart as she headed in that direction. While she drove, her mind flashed back to the last time she'd seen Logan. It had been the day that Sydney was born. A pain ripped through her chest as she remembered his cold eyes running over her with a look of disdain before dismissing her to get into the limo and drive away with Melissa Shaw.

"That was seven years ago, Hope," she said to herself when she drove into the ferry port and looked for a parking space, finding one close to the entrance. "I'm sure he doesn't even remember you or your summer fling."

She drew in a deep breath and let it out before turning off the engine and glancing at herself in the mirror, wondering if she should touch some gloss onto her lips.

"Stop it!" Hope admonished herself. "I'm sure Logan doesn't care if your lips have a gloss on them or not."

Hope took a few more deep breaths to steady her nerves before pushing her door open and climbing out of her SUV. Her legs felt wobbly, and she clenched her fists to stop her hands from shaking. Hope forced herself to walk as steadily as she could to the disembarking passenger area. She stopped when she saw the same kind of blue sedan that was parked outside her apartment the other night.

Hope was going to walk over to it, but it pulled away from the curb, made an illegal U-turn, and sped off up the road, but not before Hope managed to get a partial plate number. She frowned as she watched the car speed off, but it was soon forgotten when Hope saw people starting to disembark from the ferry, and she hurried to the waiting area.

She stood to one side, watching the passengers exit the ferry and walk to the exit gate. Logan was taller than most people on the ferry, and Hope immediately spotted him. Her heart went wild the moment he lifted his head and looked around the port. Hope's first instinct was to duck and hide, but she reminded herself she was there to take him home. She clenched her jaw and shook her head, breathing out before stepping forward as Logan cleared the gate.

"Logan!" Hope's voice unintentionally snapped through the air like a crack of a whip.

She drew more than his attention to her, making her cheeks heat as she wished the ground would open up and swallow her. Especially when her eyes met Logan's, who had stopped dead in his tracks and was staring at her with narrowed eyes.

Shoot! Hope admonished herself. *What the heck, Hope!* Other than being able to rewind time, there was nothing to do about her shrill tone when she'd called out to him. All she could do was brush it off and move forward.

"Hope?" Logan's voice was deep and gravelly before he cleared his throat. "This is a surprise."

Her eyes dropped to the cane he used as he walked awkwardly towards her with a large duffel bag slung over his shoulder.

"Sorry about screaming across the docks." Hope felt her cheeks grow hotter as she apologized for the way she'd called him. "I'm here to take you home because your grandparents are at the cardiologist in Bangor, and Thorn is in the countryside, tending to sick cattle."

Good grief, Hope, stop babbling! she thought to herself.

"Oh!" Logan's eyebrows shot up in surprise. "Why are my grandparents at the cardiologist's?"

Oh great! Hope thought. *He didn't know about his grandfather's heart condition.* This was turning out to be a great first meeting.

"Your grandfather's gone for a check-up," Hope told him. "They are both still fit and on the go as ever."

"I guess now that you own the bakery across the street from my grandparents' stores, you see them all the time?" Logan followed Hope as she started walking towards her car.

Hope looked at him, unsure how to answer that· before deciding it wasn't a lie. She did see Lavinia and Rod nearly every day at the store.

"Yes, I see them at the store," Hope confirmed. "I buy a lot of my fresh herbs from your grandfather now that he's started growing his own."

"Really?" Logan pulled an impressed face. "I know he always wanted to grow his own herbs, but my grandmother was against him digging up her perfect garden."

"They bought some of the open land next to their house." Hope laughed because she knew how protective Lavinia was over her perfect garden. "He grows a lot of his own fresh produce now. Especially since that farm he used to get his from is now a horse ranch."

"No, kidding?" Logan looked at her, surprised. "That's a shame. They supplied nearly the entire island with fresh herbs and produce."

They stopped at Hope's car. She opened the SUV's trunk and looked at his large duffel bag.

"Is that your only luggage?" Hope realized she should've asked when they were back at the ferry.

"Yup," Logan confirmed. "This is how I travel these days." He laughed softly as he stuffed the bag into the trunk and pushed it closed.

Hope walked to the driver's side of the car while Logan walked to the passenger side, and they climbed into the car. Hope had backed out of the parking and was on her way towards the Hall's house before either of them spoke again.

"This was very kind of you to get me, Hope," Logan looked at her. "Thank you."

"Of course," Hope stammered and gave him a tight smile. "Your grandparents told me you were home for good?"

"Yes," Logan said with a nod, looking out the side window as he spoke. "It's the life of a civilian for me now."

There was an edge to his voice that made Hope glance at him. He turned and caught her eyes for a second.

"I guess it can't be easy for you," Hope said softly, her voice filled with compassion.

"Without my parents constantly hounding me and trying to get me to attend celebrity functions," Logan told her. "It's going to be a lot easier being back home."

"Well, I know your grandparents are so excited to have you back with them," Hope assured him.

"How are you, Hope?" Logan changed the subject, surprising her by turning it to her.

"I…." Hope was taken off guard by his question and the look of genuine interest in his eyes. "I have the bakery now." She said stupidly, knowing he was still in touch with Chase, who would've already told him that.

"I know," Logan said. "Chase tells me you've expanded it into a bigger coffee shop and a catering and event planning business."

"That's right." Hope nodded. "Life's been hectic for me."

"I can imagine." Logan turned and looked at her. She could feel his eyes on her, and she glanced nervously at him. "I believe you have a daughter."

Hope got such a fright when he spoke about Sydney that she nearly drove them into a ditch.

"Careful!" Logan instinctively reached for the wheel.

His hand grabbed hers, and electricity shot up her arm. Hope had to force herself to hold the wheel steady and not swerve them off the road again.

"Sorry," Hope said, grateful when he drew his hand back. "I thought I saw a rabbit."

You thought you saw a rabbit? Hope gave herself a mental shake and was grateful as they arrived at the gates to the Hall estate.

"Ah, home sweet home," Logan said softly, his attention drawn to the gates.

"Yes, welcome home." Hope leaned through the window and punched the code into the gate security keypad without thinking.

"I see my grandparents must really trust you if they gave you the code to the front gates," Logan noted.

"Uh...." Hope sat back and closed her window as the gates slid open. "I..." She cleared her throat as her mind raced, looking for an excuse for why she'd have the gate code. "I do a lot of deliveries for them." It wasn't a lie.

"Oh, that's nice of you." Logan smiled. "Thank you for helping them."

"Of course," Hope said, her heart hammering in her chest. She hated talking in half-truths.

As they pulled up to the front stairs, the doors opened, and Cindy rushed out of the house to greet Logan and help him with his bag. After climbing out of the car and greeting Cindy, Logan leaned back into the car.

"Thank you again, Hope," Logan said.

"Any time," Hope told him and wanted to kick herself.

"I may take you up on that," Logan warned, giving her a smile before closing the door.

Hope watched him walk up the stairs to the front door, where he turned and waved her off. As Hope drove out the front gates of the Hall estate, she stopped to steady her beating heart and shake out her tingling hands. Hope had been gripping the steering wheel so tight to keep her hands steady they'd gotten pins and needles in them.

"Well, that was the first Logan encounter over and done with," Hope said to herself as she pulled onto the road and headed for the bakery. "Let's hope there's not too many more."

But as she drove back towards town, she knew that was wishful thinking. Bar Harbor wasn't that big, and Logan would take over his grandparent's store across the road from her bakery. The time for getting in front of the truth was running out. Hope had to decide how she was going to deal with it. Hope was so deep in thought that she nearly didn't see the white horse and its rider dash onto the road. She slammed on the brakes and swerved to the side, missing the horse by mere inches.

Hope sat catching her breath as waves of shock washed over her.

"What on earth is a horse doing on this road?" Hope spluttered furiously, getting out of the car as the rider came up behind her and slid off the horse.

"Are you crazy?" A familiar female voice screamed at her. "You nearly killed me and my prize stallion."

Hope's jaw dropped as she spun around. Just when she thought the worst part of her day was over, she came face to face with Melissa Shaw.

CHAPTER FOUR

Logan threw his duffel bag onto the floor of his bedroom suite in his family home and plopped down onto the king-sized bed. It was so good to be home. Although Logan would've preferred to have been prepared for it, he was glad his first meeting with Hope was over.

He drew in a shaky breath and pinched the bridge of his nose. Why must Hope be so beautiful, kind, and caring? Well, at least to other people, she was kind and caring. Logan reminded himself that Hope hadn't given a second thought to ripping his heart out and stomping on it. Still, Hope was being good to his grandparents, who, even if they didn't like to admit it, were getting on in their years and needed all the help they could get.

Thinking about his grandparents, Logan picked up his phone and called his grandmother because his grandfather never answered his phone.

"Hello, my boy," Lavinia cheerily answered her phone on the third ring. "Are you at home, and did Thorn get there on time? I know he can be quite absent-minded when he's working."

"Hi, Gran," Logan greeted her back. "I'm home, and I was picked up on time. Thank you for organizing that for me."

Logan left off who brought him home.

"Your grandfather and I are sorry we can't be there. But this appointment came up at the last minute, and we had to take it, or your grandfather would have to wait another four months," Lavinia explained. "I wish there was another cardiologist as good as Doctor Gold around these parts. The man is so terribly busy."

"I understand, Gran," Logan assured her. "Why is Granddad seeing a cardiologist?" He frowned worriedly. "Is he alright?"

"He had that scare last October when he landed in the hospital after having a heart attack," Lavinia told him. "Don't you ....." She trailed off and stopped. "Of course." She paused again. "I'm sorry. I forgot that was the week you were injured."

"No one told me about Granddad because I was injured?" Logan's voice was laced with anger and shock at having learned his grandfather had a heart attack that he knew nothing about.

"Your mother thought it was best not to say anything, sweetheart," Lavinia told him.

"So, she just never told me after that?" Logan asked in disbelief. "How is he really?"

"He is fine," Lavinia assured Logan. "As fit as possible, he followed the doctor's orders. We're just here for a checkup. You know all the follow-up blood pressure checks, blood tests, kidney function, cholesterol, and medication review."

"That's a relief, Gran." Logan realized then he'd been holding his breath listening to his grandmother while his whole body tingled with fright. "Why would my mother not want me to know about Granddad?"

"She didn't want to worry you, honey," Lavinia told him.

They chatted for a few more minutes before saying goodbye and ending the call.

He sat down on his bed and sighed in relief as a peaceful silence descended on him. The constant unease Logan had felt in the pit of his stomach while he was in California with his parents had gone. Well, now that Hope was gone, and he knew his grandfather was alright, the feeling had subsided. Logan's phone rang, drawing him out of his thoughts. He picked it up and saw that it was one of his best friends, Rose Davenport.

"Hi, Rose," Logan sang into the phone, happy to hear from her.

"Hey, you," Rose's soft voice drifted through the receiver. "I was checking in to see if you got to Bar Harbor safely."

"You would've known that as soon as I stepped ashore if you'd fetched me from the ferry," Logan pointed out.

"I'm sorry about that," Rose said. "My mother has asked me to help the local dentist at the old age home, and right now, I'm up to my elbows in false teeth and gums."

Logan laughed, "I would offer to help," he retorted. "But you know how I feel about digging around in people's mouths."

"Yes, you wouldn't even help me pull my last baby tooth out when we were younger," Rose remembered. "You nor Chase had the guts to do it."

"As I recall, you did just fine with that tooth alone." Logan grinned as he remembered he and Chase had nearly fainted at the sight of all the blood from that tooth had caused Rose.

"Enough about my baby teeth," Rose moved the conversation on. "Do you want to meet for lunch?"

"I would love to," Logan accepted her invitation. "But you'll have to get me as I can't drive."

"I know," Rose's voice dropped. "I'll be at your place around twelve?"

"That sounds awesome," Logan told her. "I look forward to catching up."

"Me too," Rose said. "I must go." She hung up.

Later that morning, Logan was about to go downstairs when his phone rang. It was Chase.

"Hey," Logan said, answering the phone.

"Hi," Chase greeted him. "How's it feel to be back in Bar Harbor?"

"I haven't really gone anywhere yet, but it is so peaceful being back at my grandparent's house," Logan told him. "How is California?"

"As exciting as ever," Chase said with a laugh. "I wanted to let you know that I'm coming home for five days from Thursday."

"Which is tomorrow," Logan pointed out.

"I've spoken to my mother, and we're going to have a Wright family and friends barbeque on Sunday," Chase told him. "So don't make any plans for that day."

"I'm putting it in my diary as we speak," Logan joked. "I've missed the Wright family and friends barbecues."

"You can't go wrong with a Wright barbecue." Chase laughed. "My mother wants my sister to cater it, and I was hoping you could help her."

"I'm sure Hope doesn't need my help catering," Logan's heart thudded in his chest as his mind skidded back to the last event they'd done together seven years ago.

"Oh, not with the pastries and food, but my mother needs a new barbecue grill, wood for the fire pit, tables, and so on," Chase said. "I'll only get in late tomorrow, and as you know, I'm hopeless at organizing events."

"Well, you speak to Hope about the barbecue, and *you* let her know that I'll be helping with getting it all setup," Logan told Chase. "I'm sure you can borrow my grandparents' grill if your mother no longer has one." He walked to his bedroom window and looked at the perfectly manicured lawn. His eyes settled on the covered patio where they kept the grill that had never been used.

"I think my mother wants to buy a new one. She just hasn't gotten around to it," Chase told him. "You're much better at picking those things out than my mother or me."

"Sure," Logan agreed.

They chatted about the weekend for a few more minutes before saying their goodbyes and hanging up. Logan stood staring at his phone for a few minutes, not believing he'd gotten himself roped into helping Chase organize a barbecue over the weekend.

"So much for keeping a low profile and having a nice relaxing time." Logan sighed, picking up his walking cane and heading for the stairs.

When he got to the bottom of the stairs, his eyes widened as he heard Cindy arguing with someone at the front door. Logan suddenly realized he had told her that he wouldn't be disturbed and didn't want any visitors. He had forgotten to tell her that Rose was picking him up for lunch. Logan walked as quickly as he could to the front door and froze when he saw who Cindy was arguing with.

"Melissa?" Logan scowled. "What are you doing here?"

"There you are, darling," Melissa drawled. "Cindy won't let me see you."

"I told her I didn't want to be disturbed," Logan told her, then looked at Cindy. "It's okay, I've got this."

"You have a guest in the living room when you're done here," Cindy whispered before nodding and leaving him with an irate Melissa.

"Are you going to ask me in?" Melissa gave him a saucy smile as he blocked her entrance.

"I'm sorry, but I'm on my way out," Logan's eyes narrowed. "Why are you here, Melissa?"

"Your mother thought you might get lonely back in Bar

Harbor," Melissa purred and reached out to straighten the lapel of his cotton shirt.

Logan stepped back out of her reach, annoyance flooding him. "Well, my mother was wrong," he told her. "I'm sorry, Melissa, but I don't have time to visit today."

"Really?" Melissa pouted prettily and batted her eyelashes. "Not even with me?"

"Especially not with you," Logan hissed. "I'm sorry you wasted your time coming to Bar Harbor, but I can assure you I won't be alone or lonely."

Logan took a step forward, making her step back to get her out of the doorway.

"Darling, I've been patient and waited for you to recover," Melissa's tone changed as she snapped. "Don't you think it's time we talked about your rash decision about us breaking up before you went on that dangerous mission?"

"It wasn't a rash decision, Melissa," Logan assured her. "It had been coming for a good few years." He looked pointedly at his wristwatch once again. "I'm sorry, but I have to go."

He stepped back to close the door, but she stopped him.

"So your plans are more important than me and our relationship?" Melissa looked at him in surprise. "You were serious, weren't you?" Her voice dropped, and her eyes started to sparkle with unshed tears.

"If you mean when I say we're over for good this time?" Logan looked at her. "Then yes, I meant it." He sighed and ran a hand through his hair. "Look, Melissa, you and I both know what we had wasn't real. It was merely for your image, and while my mother thought I was with you, she stopped trying to set me up every time I visited them."

"Your mother tried to set you up with another woman knowing we were together?" Melissa's eyes flashed with hurt for a few seconds but were quickly replaced by anger.

"Please don't twist my words to suit yourself," Logan pinched the bridge of his nose as he tried to keep from getting angry. "And don't come here shouting at my grandparent's staff. They are only following my instructions."

"You really don't want to see me?" Melissa looked at him in disbelief. "I was hoping you'd come to your senses now that—" she looked at his walking cane and the side that took the worst of his injuries. "That you are on your way to recovery."

"I came to my senses eleven months ago, Melissa," Logan assured her. "You and I are over and will never be a couple again." He glanced behind her and saw a sleek silver Maserati parked in the drive that he presumed was hers. "I really have to go."

"You're going to regret this!" Melissa's eyes narrowed as she glared at him.

"No, I don't think I will," Logan told her. "It's what I should've done years ago."

Melissa gave him one last scathing look before spinning on her heels and stomping off. To his surprise, she walked past the Maserati and disappeared toward the side of the house. Logan frowned and shrugged, thinking she must've parked near the garages before he closed the front door.

"Wow!" Rose's voice had him spinning around. "America's sweetheart is about as sour as a bag of sour patch kids." She gave a low whistle. "If only her fans knew the real Melissa."

"How long have you been standing there?" Logan stared at his friend.

"I haven't been standing here," Rose pointed to where she was leaning against the living room door frame. "I was hiding in the living room." She grinned. "Just close enough to the door to hear what was going on but not close enough to be seen." She shuddered. "Melissa does not like me."

"She is jealous of your natural beauty and grace," Logan told his friend as she walked toward him with her arms open wide to hug him. He enfolded her in his arms, kissing her rich deep red hair. "Hi, Rose."

"Hi, you." Rose kissed his cheek before running her fingers over its burn scar. "I'm glad you're still with us."

"I am, too," Logan told her. "Now, are we going to eat? I haven't eaten since early this morning, and I'm starving."

They left the house and walked down the steps, and to his surprise, Rose walked around to the driver's side door of the silver Maserati.

"This is yours?" Logan stood staring at the magnificent car in surprise.

"Yup!" Rose nodded. "I got it in the divorce." She grinned, sliding into the car, and Logan climbed into the passenger seat, admiring the beautiful craftsmanship of the interior.

"You took the man's car?" Logan glanced at her.

"He was the one that was cheating on me," Rose pointed out. "And it wasn't the first time either." She buckled up before starting the engine, which roared to life.

"And you're comfortable driving this car?" Logan looked at her in surprise.

"Yup!" Rose pulled the car around the fountain in the middle of the driveway and coasted towards the gates. "It handles beautifully."

"I must admit to being really impressed, Rose," Logan ran his hand over the plush leather seats. "You went from being nervous to drive a car to driving a supercar."

"I was so mad at Richard when he bought this car," Rose remembered. "But after I'd driven it a few times, I fell in love with it, and soon, I drove it more than he did." She signed and ran her hand over the dashboard. "I got Hilda in the divorce settlement."

"You named an Italian supercar Hilda?" Logan choked.

"What's wrong with Hilda?" She looked at him with narrowed eyes.

"Nothing, it's just not the name I'd give this car." Logan held out his hand expressively.

Before Logan could say anymore, he was jolted forward as Rose slammed on the brakes.

"What the heck!" Rose hissed.

Logan lifted his head as a huge white horse reared in front of them while the rider battled to settle the stallion.

"Are horses even allowed on this road?" Logan asked as tiny shock waves zapped through his nervous system.

"I'm sure they are not!" Rose's eyes flashed with anger as she pulled the car over.

The rider managed to calm the horse down, and they were both amazed to see Melissa in the saddle. They were about to leave the car when she glared at them, kicked the horse into a gallop, and sped away. They were quiet for a few seconds as they watched the horse disappear towards the Riddle estate, a few houses down from Logan's.

"So that's how she got to my house," Logan realized. "I hope the horse didn't get into my grandmother's flower beds."

"Or poop on her lawn!" Rose pulled her chin back and raised her eyebrows before they looked at each other and laughed. "What on earth is wrong with that woman?"

She turned the car on and pulled onto the road before taking the turn off that headed out of town.

"Where are we going?" Logan looked at Rose, ignoring her last question and thinking it safer to change the subject. Rose and Chase had never liked Melissa nor believed her sweet facade.

"Remember the Ware's farm on the outskirts of town?" Rose asked him.

"Yes." Logan nodded.

"Old Mr. Ware died and left the farm to his sister's son Mike Taylor," Rose told him. "Mike has turned the place into a dude ranch and has opened a Wares Mixed Cuisine restaurant on it."

They arrived at the ranch ten minutes later and pulled

into a parking space. They were walking toward the door to the restaurant when Logan stopped dead in his tracks as he saw Hope walk out the door laughing with a tall, dark-haired man.

"Thanks, Mike," Hope walked towards a pink van with a pretty white sign, Cookie Dough Bakery. She opened the back doors, and Mike, carrying a few crates for her, slid them into the back and then closed the doors for her. "I'll bring your special order on Saturday. I'm not sure if Sally will be back at work. She is not very well, I'm afraid."

"Oh, that's a shame," Mike looked disappointed. "Send her my regards."

"I will do, Mike—" Hope stopped short when her eyes met Logan's.

"Hello, again," Logan greeted her.

"Hi," Hope said before her eyes slid toward Rose. "Hello, Rose."

"Hello, Hope." Rose's eyes narrowed questioningly. "Please tell me you dropped off your cherry toffee cheesecake."

"She sure did," Mike answered for Hope with a laugh. "Hi, you must be Logan Hall."

Mike, who topped Logan's six foot by a good two inches, stepped forward and held out his hand to Logan.

"Yes," Logan said, taking the man's hand and shaking it.

"I'm Mike Taylor," Mike introduced himself.

After introductions, Hope started walking towards the driver's side of the bakery van.

"I must get going. I have to get Sydney from school early today," Hope said. "I'll see you on Saturday morning Mike." She looked at Rose and Logan. "Enjoy your lunch. You won't be disappointed with Mike's food."

Logan couldn't think of anything to say, so he nodded and waved as she buckled up and drove away. His heart was thudding in his chest, like he'd just run a marathon, as he pictured how beautiful and carefree she'd looked, laughing up at Mike when she walked out the door. Something twanged inside him as a wave of jealousy hit him, and his eyes dropped to Mike's hand. There was no ring on the man's finger.

"Come in." Mike broke into his thoughts. "I've put you at your usual table, Rose."

"Thank you, Mike," Rose preceded the men into a brightly lit room.

She walked over to a secluded booth at the far side of the restaurant next to a large window that looked out over a rolling lawn to a sparkling lake. Horses grazed lazily in the afternoon sun, swishing the flies and critters off their bodies with their long tails.

"This is really nice," Logan said, sliding into the plush leather booth in front of Rose and putting his cane beside him.

"Are you okay?" Rose looked at him.

"Yes, why wouldn't I be?" Logan gave her a smile hoping it didn't look false or give away how rattled he was at seeing Hope with Mike.

"So far, you've had quite the day running into Melissa," Rose smiled at the waiter who brought them their menus.

"Oh, I just ignore her." Logan shook his head. "I just wonder why she's being so pushy about us getting back together all of a sudden."

"Yes, me too," Rose said. "I hope this time that you don't give in to pressure from her or your mother and let Melissa clean up her own mess."

"I intend to," Logan assured her and then frowned. "Have you ever heard of a private security company called Crow?"

"Why would I know about a private security company?" Rose frowned.

"Because your father had a private security company, and I wondered if you'd know," Logan shrugged.

"Sorry I wasn't eavesdropping," Mike stopped by with a

plate of hors d'oeuvres. "I just wanted to bring you a complimentary hors d'oeuvres platter."

"It looks delicious," Rose said as Mike slid the platter onto their table.

"Thank you," Mike looked at Logan. "I'm surprised you don't know who Crow Private Security is."

"Why would I know?" Logan looked at him, confused.

Mike frowned as he looked at Logan. "Because your family owns it, and they do a lot of private security for celebrities and other high-profile clients."

CHAPTER FIVE

Hope was rattled after bumping into Logan. Fate really was having a field day with her dilemma. She was so deep in thought she found herself on the way to the bakery instead of Sydney's school. The principal had called her while she was making the delivery at Mike's restaurant because Sydney wasn't feeling well.

"I'm a terrible mother!" Hope breathed before turning the bakery van around and heading for Bar Harbor Elementary School. "You need to get Logan Hall out of your mind, Hope." She pulled into a parking space in the school's parking lot. "He's distracting you from the important things in your life."

Hope grabbed her purse and hopped out of the van. As she swung the door closed, it caught her purse, yanking it from her hands and knocking it to the ground.

"Oh, shoot!" Hope hissed.

As she bent down to pick it up, a movement near the bushes behind the parking lot caught her eye. She stood, looked towards it, and could've sworn she saw someone with a camera disappear behind the giant oak tree near the bushes.

"What the—" Hope squinted into the distance, where she could see a glint from behind the tree.

Anger spurted through her when she scanned the parking lot and saw the same type of blue sedan that had been parked by her apartment near the back of the car park. The front plate matched the partial she'd managed to get earlier that day. Hope scooped up her purse, took out her phone, and zoomed in on the car, ensuring she could read the license plate before taking a photo. She went onto her messaging app and sent the vehicle picture to a friend in the FBI.

"Hopefully, I'll soon know who you are, stalker." Hope glanced in the direction of the tree one last time.

If Sydney didn't have a bad stomach ache, Hope would've marched over to the man and demanded to know why he was following her, even if it was a bad idea. Hope had been on eggshells since Lavinia told her Logan was coming home. Her plan to avoid him had failed horribly when she'd already encountered Logan twice that day. Hope spun around and rushed into the school heading for the nurse's office, where the principal told her Sydney was. As Hope raised her hand and brought it down to knock on the door, it was yanked open by the new school nurse, who Hope nearly struck on the forehead. The woman managed to dodge the hit.

"I'm sorry," Hope breathed, alarmed that she'd nearly unintentionally hit the new school nurse in the head.

"It's okay," the young nurse told Hope. "I realize you were about to knock on my door, not my head." She grinned. "I'm Harriet Lovell, and you must be Sydney's mother?"

"Yes, I'm Hope," she introduced herself, looking at the nurse with worry for her daughter coursing through her veins. "The principal told me that Sydney is not well and has a bad stomach ache."

"She does," Harriet confirmed. "She started vomiting a few moments before you got here."

Hope's eyes widened worriedly. "Where is she?"

"This way." Harriet led Hope to Sydney's room.

"Mommy," Sydney wailed as Hope rushed to her side.

"Hey, baby, mommy's here." Hope brushed a few stray strands of hair from Sydney's forehead. "Are you able to stand up?"

Sydney nodded as Harriet helped her sit up. "I might get sick, though."

"That's okay. I have a bag for your mother to take in the car with you," Harriet told them, helping Sydney off the bed. "I think instead of walking to the car, you let me push you in the wheelchair."

Sydney let Nurse Harriet lead her to the wheelchair and settle her into it. On the way out of the nurse's office, she grabbed a bag and handed it to her in case she felt sick in the car.

"I need to sign Sydney out of school," Hope remembered when they were halfway down the hall.

"We'll wait near the front steps," Harriet told her.

Hope nodded, turned, and rushed to the administration office, where she signed Sydney out of the school. While Harriet helped Sydney into the car, Hope glanced around the parking lot and noticed the blue sedan was gone. Once Harriet had Sydney buckled up in the back with a sick bag on her lap, Hope thanked her before calling Doctor Meldan. Hope was told to bring Sydney in right away. They would squeeze her in between appointments. As soon as she hung up, she pulled out of the parking lot and headed toward the hospital.

"Why are we going to the hospital and not the doctor, Mommy?" Sydney asked her mother wearily. "I don't want to stay there overnight again."

Hope looked at her daughter in the mirror and saw the panic in her eyes.

"Doctor Meldan's offices are now in the new building across from the hospital, honey," Hope told her. "We're not going into the hospital section."

"Okay," Sydney said, relieved.

"Are you going to be okay walking?" Hope asked Sydney ten minutes later as she pulled into a parking space in front of the new building across the car park from the hospital.

"Yes, I think so," Sydney told her. "I'll have to bring the sick bag, though, because I think I'm going to throw up again." She swallowed, and as Hope turned around in her seat to look at her daughter, she threw up into the sick bag.

"Oh, honey," Hope breathed, feeling for her child.

Hope unbuckled her seatbelt and climbed out of her car before helping her daughter. She managed to get Sydney into the doctor's office before she got sick again. The nurse took them into one of the exam rooms and gave Sydney a blue emesis bag if she got sick again.

It wasn't long until the doctor saw them and told Hope Sydney had a stomach bug. It was going around at the schools, and he'd had a wave of school kids in that week. He prescribed some medicine and gave Sydney an injection to stop the nausea and pain. He wrote a note excusing her from school until Wednesday, which Sydney was happy about.

Hope took Sydney home and put her to bed with Barbie on the floor. She was barely out the door when her daughter fell asleep. Hope stopped and smiled at her baby girl. Her heart felt so heavy when her child was sick and helpless because there was nothing she could do but be there to ensure she got her medicine. Hope wished there was a way she could take on the illness for her daughter.

She quietly pulled the bedroom door leaving it slightly open and walked away when her phone rang. Hope pulled it out of her pocket and saw it was her second eldest brother, Chase.

"Hello, Chase," Hope kept her voice low until she was on her way down the stairs and heading toward the bakery entrance.

"Hi, little sister," Chase chirped. "How are things going in Bar Harbor?"

"They were going okay until Sydney got sick today," Hope told him.

"Oh, no," Chase became serious. "What's wrong?"

Hope told him what the doctor had said.

"She's sleeping now," Hope told him.

"I'm sorry to hear my favorite girl is sick," Chase said. "Send her my love and tell her I'll bring her something special from Los Angeles."

"I'll tell her you send your love." Hope opened the bakery door and walked into the kitchen. "How are things in California?"

"As hectic as ever," Chase answered. "I'm calling to let you know I'll be home for a few days. I will arrive tomorrow afternoon."

"Oh!" Hope's eyes widened in surprise. "Is there any special reason you're coming home at such short notice?" Her eyes narrowed suspiciously. "Are you hiding from a mobster?"

"What?" Chase sounded shocked. "No!" He laughed. "Why on earth would you think that?"

"I don't know," Hope said, raising her hand. "You work with a lot of shady rappers."

"They're not shady," Chase defended his clients.

"Really?" Hope's brow crinkled. "At least three of the clients I know you represent have records longer than both Thorn's arms when he has them held out."

"That doesn't make them shady," Chase pointed out. "They made some bad choices in their life, and they pay me to help them back onto the right path."

"You mean to cover up their mess and then make it disappear." Hope greeted her kitchen employees before going into her office.

"How did we get onto my shady clients?" Chase asked her and stopped before realizing what he'd just said.

"See, even you admit they're shady." Hope laughed, picturing him rolling his eyes. "But, regardless of why you're coming home for a few days, I look forward to seeing you."

"To be honest," Chase's voice dropped. "I'm looking forward to a few days' break."

There was a catch in his voice that made Hope frown. "Are you okay?"

"Just tired from working so hard," Chase breathed. "I wanted to ask you something, but now I feel bad doing so because Syd's sick."

"What is it?" Hope sat in her office chair and switched on her computer to check her calendar and orders.

"I've kind of planned a Wright family and friend barbecue for Sunday," Chase told her.

"Oh!" Hope's brows shot up as she tilted her head to hook the phone between her ear and shoulder as she typed. "I take it you're staying with Mom? And if so, does she know about your plans?"

"Yes, I'm staying with Mom," Chase confirmed. "And, yes, I asked first this time."

"And she agreed?" Hope logged into the system, then put her phone on her desk and switched it to speakerphone as she opened her calendar to Sunday. "Because Sydney doesn't have dog training lessons this week, we can make the barbecue if she's well enough."

"Of course," Chase agreed. "But ...."

Before he said another word, Hope realized why Chase was really calling her, "You want me to cater for your barbecue."

"If you can," Chase said quickly. "Mom checked to see if you had anything else you were catering for on Sunday, and she said your day was clear. I didn't know Sydney was going to be ill." He went quiet for a few seconds. "So I'll understand if you can't make a few of your delicious salads and finger foods." He paused again. "And if you can, maybe some of your tempting treats for dessert."

"You said you had Mom check my calendar?" Hope's eyes fell on a sticky note that had fallen off her monitor, and she picked it up.

"I did, sorry," Chase apologized. "I don't know if you know this." He cleared his throat. "But Logan is back in Bar Harbor, and one of our informal gatherings will be a nice welcome home for him."

The mention of Logan's name made her nerve endings prickle, jolting her heart. "I'll see what I can do because I have a kid's birthday party. I have to make a cake and cupcakes for it."

"Thank you," Chase sang into the phone. "Oh, and because I'm the one doing the inviting, I've asked Logan to help you organize a new grill for Mom, tables, chairs, wood for the fire pit, and anything else you need."

"What?" Hope choked. "I don't need help catering a barbecue."

"I know," Chase said defensively. "But Logan loves organizing these things, and I'm trying to help him fit back into civilian life."

"That's sweet of you." Hope felt her heart twinge for them both. Chase may lead a work-a-holic playboy life, but he was always loyal and fiercely protective over his loved ones. "I'll speak to Logan about anything Mom may need for the barbecue."

"Thank you, you are my favorite sister by far!" Chase told her.

"Sure," Hope sighed and rolled her eyes. "Who is picking you up from the ferry port tomorrow?"

"Rose," Chase answered. "She's taking Logan and me out for dinner after I've dropped my stuff off at Mom's house."

"I think Rose just loves showing off her new toy," Hope didn't mean what she'd said to sound as spiteful as it did.

"Are you jealous of her car?" Chase teased.

"Not at all," Hope denied. "I wouldn't want to drive a supercar. I prefer my sturdy SUV and delivery van."

"Oh, darn," Chase breathed. "I have to go. I've got a meeting."

They said their goodbyes and hung up. Hope dropped her head into her hands and ran her fingers through her hair.

"This day just gets better and better," Hope mumbled.

"Hope," Clair Wright's voice echoed through the kitchen. "Honey, are you here?"

Hope dropped her head back, closed her eyes, and breathed before sticking her head out her office door. "I'm here, Mom."

"Hi, honey," Clair glided to her, kissing Hope on the cheek. "Why do you look so flushed?" She glanced into Hope's office. "Do you still not have air conditioning in here?"

"I have air conditioning in my office, Mom," Hope assured her mother. "Not that I don't love your visits." Her eyes narrowed. "But I have a busy afternoon."

"I heard that Sydney was brought home ill and wanted to check up on my granddaughter," Clair told her.

"She's upstairs asleep." Hope stepped back into her office so her mother could enter. "But I have a feeling your visit is not just about Sydney."

Hope sat in her chair while her mother sat in front of her.

"I did want to check in on you and find out how you were coping with Logan being back in town," Clair said.

"I'm fine, Mom," Hope assured her, and her eyes narrowed suspiciously as she looked at her mother. "How did you get here?"

"I drove—" Clair pursed her lips, realizing too late what she'd done. "Okay, so you caught me."

"Did you, Thorn, Lavinia, and Ron plan on having me get Logan?" Hope glared at her.

"Honey," Claire sat forward in the chair. "There was a cancellation that allowed Ron to see his doctor in Bangor earlier." She bit her bottom lip. "And I may have convinced Thorn to call you and ask you to get Logan." She held up her hand, stopping Hope from saying more. "But Thorn really did have to go out of town to tend to sick cattle, and my car does need to go in for a service, but it's only going in tomorrow."

"Why would you do that to me?" Hope looked at her mother in disbelief. "You know how stressed I've been about him coming home."

"Lavinia and I thought it would be better to rip the band-aid off and get your inevitable first meeting over and done with," Clair explained. "We all saw how much you were stressing over it." She ran her eyes over her daughter. "You even lost weight and have dark circles under your eyes from lack of sleep."

"Well, thank you for that, Mother," Hope said haughtily. "That doesn't make me feel bad about my appearance at all."

"I'm sorry, honey, but you look tired and far too thin." Clair moaned at her. "We thought that putting you two together on day one would help alleviate some of the stress and anxiousness about seeing him again."

"I know you all meant well," Hope told her. "But, please, in the future, speak to me first before making plans for my day." She raised her eyebrows. "Like the Sunday barbecue I'm catering for and Logan is helping me with."

"Now, honey," Clair held up her hands and looked sideways at Hope. "I knew about the barbecue and checked your catering and event planner for anything you may have had on Sunday." She shook her head. "I never volunteered for your catering services. I told Chase he'd have to ask you, and I promise I knew nothing about Logan helping you organize it."

"I believe you." Hope sighed.

"I can speak to Chase about it," Claire offered.

"No," Hope leaned her elbows on her desk. "Chase is just trying to be nice and help Logan feel like he still fits into civilian life."

"You know, honey, if you had told Chase about Sydney...." Clair trailed off before waving her hand in the air. "I'm sure he'd never have roped you into working with Logan on Sunday."

"If I had told Chase," Hope pointed out. "We wouldn't be having this barbecue because I doubt Chase and Logan would still be friends."

"It would've blown over," Claire assured her. "Just like when the truth comes out one day, it may take a while, but it *will* blow over." She reached over and took Hope's hands in hers. "Chase may be fiercely overprotective of you, but he also has the biggest heart and has been known to be very forgiving."

"Not when it comes to something he'd see as a huge betrayal of friendship and trust," Hope reminded her mother. "Do you remember Debra Wicks?"

"Honey, Debra was a completely different situation." Clair's eyes widened at the mention of one of Chase's high school sweethearts. "She only dated Chase to get close to the Halls."

"That broke his heart and nearly ripped his friendship with Logan apart," Hope shuddered. "I remember how angry and hurt Chase had been for weeks after Debra dumped him a few days before their junior prom to be taken to the ball by Logan."

"Yes, but Logan didn't really agree to take that sneaky cow," Clair reminded Hope. "He only said he would because he was trying to get Chase to see who Debra really was."

"And look how well that ended for them," Hope said. "Chase, Rose, and Logan went to the prom together."

"Yes, but the two of them worked it out," Claire said.

"That's exactly what they will do when you tell Logan and Chase the truth."

"This is a little bit more serious than stealing a prom date, Mom," Hope pointed out and glanced at the clock on her wall. "I'm going to have to get moving." She started to stand up. "I have a final delivery, but I must check on Sydney first."

"You go make your delivery, and I'll check on my granddaughter," Clair offered. "I'll stay here until you get back."

"Thank you, Mom," Hope breathed a sigh of relief and kissed her mother's cheek. "You're a lifesaver. With Sally—" She broke off as a thought struck her. "That's probably where Sydney got this bug from." She threw her hands in the air. "Sally is at home with a stomach bug."

"Oh-no," Clair looked horrified. "Poor Sally."

"Please give Sydney a kiss for me and tell her I love her," Hope instructed. "Thank you, Mom." She grabbed her purse and the keys to the van as she rushed into the kitchen.

"I've already packed the van," Wes Lovell, her head baker, told Hope before she could ask him.

"Thank you, Wes." Hope gave him a grateful smile before rushing out the door.

Hope had just climbed into the van when her phone rang. It was Special Agent Lance Steel, who had grown up in Bar Harbor. His parents were wealthy investment bankers in the Bar Harbor elite crowd. They were gutted when they learned Lance wasn't interested in taking over the family business but wanted to join the FBI. He was the friend Hope had sent the picture of the blue sedan to.

"Hello, Lance," Hope answered her phone, pulling the car door shut. "Do you have any news for me?"

"Hello, Hope. I'm doing well, thanks for asking," Lance answered. "And how are you doing, Hope?" He mocked. "How is Sydney? What did the doctor say was wrong with her stomach?"

"I'm sorry, I'm fine. Thank you, Lance." Hope said sarcastically. "Sydney is going to be fine. She has a stomach bug." She put the key in the ignition. "Do you have any news for me?"

"The car belongs to a reporter from the Bar Harbor Daily," Lance told her. "Bradley Dane. He went to school with Chase, Rose, and Logan."

"Great!" Hope hissed. "Now I have a reporter following me around?"

"Maybe they're doing an exposé on your bakery," Lance suggested. "Do you want me to find out why he's following you around?"

"No, that's okay. Thank you, Lance," Hope said. "Now that I know he's not dangerous, a hurt pet owner, a disgruntled bakery customer, or a rival rapper, I will ask him myself."

"Just because he's a small-town reporter, Hope, it doesn't mean he's not dangerous," Lance warned her. "Be careful and keep me posted on why he's following you."

"I will," Hope promised.

"Why did you think you might be followed by a rival rapper?" Lance asked her, sounding confused. "Please tell me you haven't ditched your career to become a rapper!"

Hope laughed at the absurdity of what he'd just said, "You've heard me sing, Lance." A smile still lingered on her lips. "I'm an awkward speaker without having to try and put what I'm trying to say into a song."

"Well, that's a relief," Lance said, and she could hear the amusement in his voice. "But on the bright side. If you decided to become a rapper, you'd get a family discount for Chase's great PR skills."

Before Lance hung up, he warned Hope again to be careful approaching Bradley. Hope had just turned on her van's engine when a knock on her window frightened her. Her head snapped around, and her eyes widened when she saw a tall man with dark hair at her window.

"Can I help you?" Hope didn't open the window.

"Hope, I don't know if you remember me, but I was at school with your brother, Chase," the man told her. "My name is Bradley Danes. I'm a Bar Harbor Daily reporter and need to talk to you."

"Okay," Hope raised her voice slightly so they could talk through the window. "I'm listening."

"I'm writing an article on Logan Hall," Bradley told her while he jotted something down on a notepad he held for her to see.

We need to talk. You're being followed, and I suspect your vehicles are bugged.

CHAPTER SIX

Logan stood on the steps of his family home, leaning heavily on his cane, waving to Rose, who had dropped him off at home after their two-hour lunch. He rubbed his aching hip and stretched out his leg before turning to walk into the house.

"Did you forget we had a physio session that was supposed to start thirty minutes ago?" Wella Jones, his physiotherapist that his parents had flown to Bar Harbor to continue his sessions, stepped out of the front living room.

"Wella!" Logan said, looking at her apologetically. "I did forget. I'm sorry."

She was almost six foot tall, athletic, with ash blond hair, warm brown eyes, and dimples in her cheeks that dotted her smile. During one of their sessions, he'd been surprised to find out that Wella had studied to be a surgeon until she passed out during her first surgery when she watched her mentor cut the patient open. So, she went on to be a sports injury specialist and physiotherapist. She was beautiful with an effortless grace about her, and he could see why she was able to put herself through med school modeling.

Logan had gotten the impression that his mother didn't

like Wella. Still, she had come highly recommended by someone in his parent's celebrity circle. In the past four months, he'd been working with her, it was the most he'd improved from the previous six months working with the other high-priced medical personnel his parents had hired. Logan also always felt relaxed around Wella because she was genuine and the only one who told him the truth. He would get close to being able to walk and move normally, but he'd never be one hundred percent.

Logan would need to be careful with his left leg as it would be prone to easily breaking. He also needed to look into alternative daily routine exercises, like replacing running with a brisk walk. Logan could do light weights to exercise his legs and half of what he was used to for his upper body and arms. Wella had told him that he shouldn't risk trying to play hockey, one of his favorite sports, ever again. Logan's left leg, wrist, and shoulder were held together by pins.

"That's okay," Wella told him with a sheepish grin. "The ferry was late getting in, and I was twenty minutes late myself."

"Nice!" Logan looked at her with narrowed eyes. "Trying to make me feel awful about forgetting our session."

"You look like it's not a moment too soon either," Wella looked pointedly at his left side and how he was leaning on his cane. "Cindy showed me the room your grandparents turned into our session room." She raised her eyebrows as she led the way. "They spared no expense. It looks like a fancy doctor's room with a gym attached."

"Yes, my mother told me they had turned the gym into a therapy room because it was close to the pool, sauna, and steam room," Logan said.

"No, your grandparents had a new section built onto the gym, especially for the room," Wella corrected him as they walked through the entertainment area and games room to the pool. "Here we go."

They had walked past the glassed-off gym area to the one side of the indoor pool to a new section. The room was also glassed off, but heavy blinds were currently drawn, blocking the view to the pool section. Wella pushed the door open and preceded him in.

"Oh, wow!" Logan gave a low whistle. "I'll get changed and be right back."

He was about to turn and leave when Wella stopped him.

"Your grandmother ensured all your preferred physio session clothes were stocked up." Wella pointed to the pigeonholes on one side of the room. "You can close the curtains around the recovery bed while I prepare the equipment."

Logan nodded and went to change. For the next hour, he worked with Wella sweating through the pain that still burned through him at some of the simplest movements. It made him angry and frustrated at himself. It had been ten months since Logan had been injured. He shouldn't still have to rely on a cane to walk. After the session, Logan stripped off his t-shirt and dived into the pool for a few laps.

On his last lap, he dove beneath the water's surface, emerging on the pool's shallow end where Wella sat on the edge of a lounge chair watching him. He rose out of the water and stood up in the pool. Water droplets rolled down his chiseled torso, dripping into the dented welts. An angry network of scars splattered across the left side of his body. Logan breathed heavily, trying to quell the pain shooting through him, and he forced himself to steady the slight tremor starting in his leg. Logan could see the mix of admiration and concern in Wella's eyes as she watched him.

"I do marvel at your determination to push through the agony of each physio session, Logan," Wella told him. "But I have to admit to being worried." Her eyes narrowed. "I thought coming home to Bar Harbor would slow you down and lift the pressure you were feeling from your parents."

Concern furrowed her brow. "Only you seem even more determined, frustrated, and impatient with yourself than you were back there." Her jaw clenched for a few minutes. "And that's not a good thing."

"It's been ten months, Wella," Logan growled angrily, slapping the water in frustration. "I shouldn't still be dependent on a cane. I should be walking without it by now."

He wiped the water running into his eyes and pushed his wet hair back.

"Logan, you shouldn't be walking so soon after the injuries you sustained at this stage," Wella pointed out. "The progress I have witnessed you making in these past four months since I've been your physio is remarkable." Her brow knit tightly together.

Logan let out a frustrated sigh. "I know, I know. But I feel like I'm stuck in this stage of my progression." He looked at her. "You know, I watch people move about so freely, unaided, and without pain splintering through their feet with each step." He ran his hand through his wet hair and gave a mocking laugh. "I've never been one to be envious of others." He shook his head and swallowed down the burning in his chest. "But what I wouldn't give to be able to move freely again." His head tilted back, and he eyed the ceiling. "I would never take how much being able to do something as simple as bend down to tie my shoes for granted again."

Wella nodded sympathetically. "It's normal to feel that way. But trust me, you've come a long way, and you should remember you've exceeded all expectations for your recovery by miles." She stressed again. "And that is what you need to focus on, not your perceived lack of progress."

She stood up, grabbed a towel, and walked to the pool's edge, handing it to him. She watched him rub his hair dry and dab his face with the towel.

"Why do I feel a but coming on?" Logan's eyes narrowed suspiciously at her.

"If you don't stop pushing yourself as hard as you are, Logan," Wella warned him. "You could undo all your hours of hard work, sweat, and pain." She raised her eyebrows and pursed her lips. "You must remember, progress isn't always measured in leaps and bounds. Sometimes it's the small steps that count."

Logan looked down at his feet. Both were laced with raw, angry scars from the explosion and the many subsequent surgeries. "I just want to feel normal again. I want to be able to do the things I used to do without any limitations."

Wella helped him out of the pool and touched his shoulder reassuringly. "Give yourself time, Logan. Recovery isn't a race; it's a journey. And sometimes the journey is longer than we want it to be."

"Is there a different route I could take to maybe get there just a little faster," Logan pushed his luck.

Wella looked at him in disbelief and shook her head before her eyes lit up thoughtfully. "I can understand your frustration and the need to want to feel normal again." She frowned as she watched him roll his shoulder. "So maybe it's time to try a different approach if you're feeling stuck."

"What do you mean?" Logan looked at her curiously as she pushed him onto a deck chair and manipulated the shoulder he'd been fussing with.

"Sometimes, it's not just our physical injuries holding back our progress." Wella pressed on a point that made him wince, and she changed her approach to loosening the muscle.

"Okay...." Logan wasn't sure where she was going with this conversation. Still, he'd try anything to get him a step further in his recovery.

"It wasn't just your body that was injured, Logan," Wella told him. "You need to deal with the mental and emotional scars of getting injured like you were in the line of duty."

"Are you suggesting I need therapy?" Logan spluttered angrily. "Did my mother put you up to this?"

"What?" Wella stopped her massage to look at him, perplexed. "NO!" She stressed. "This is me *advising* you on what I think would help you get through this. Not because of your family but through my experience of having gone through this with Andy."

Logan's anger immediately cooled at the disdain in her voice. He knew Wella and his mother didn't get along, and she'd never buckle to one of her schemes. Logan knew he'd lashed out because he'd shunned the idea of therapy before on the promise to seek it in the near future. But the truth was Logan barely managed to keep the door on his haunting memories bolted as it was. There were a few that slipped out beneath the cracks.

Especially at night to haunt his dreams or torment him when a horn blasted near him or someone shouted. He had no intention of rehashing that day with anyone. Besides, he wasn't sure anyone except someone in his position would understand what was happening to him. It wasn't what had happened to him that haunted his dreams and tormented him. The danger becomes part of you as you become immune to it, and that wasn't his first mission or the first time he'd been exposed to a bomb blast. You're taught to deal with a lot of things as a SEAL as well as mental toughness. But they don't teach you how to deal with life after being a SEAL or.... Logan shook himself from his thoughts.

"I don't want to delve into the past, Wella," Logan told her. "I just want to move forward."

"You know, Logan," Wella's eyes narrowed as she stepped away from him. "You don't have to delve into the past or what happened with a therapist. But you can talk to them about the present and what you are so afraid of about your future that it's holding you back in more ways than one."

Logan's eyes widened with surprise at her words and perception. Of course, she would be perceptive. It wasn't only her partner that she'd been through this with. Wella had worked with many vets and people who'd been through trauma in her career. He remembered one of the first things Wella had said to him when he'd started working with her.

Recovery wasn't always a linear path. There were many facets, twists, and turns to it, and they came with good days, bad days, and the ones in between. Even something as simple as a sprained toe could have more profound complications. It's how the toe was hurt and its effect on the person. For instance, the person could've been running from someone terrible, and when they sprained their toe, they nearly died because it slowed them down. So now it's no longer just sprained toe. There are mental and emotional complications attached to the injury.

Logan realized now that Wella had been referring to his injuries as having a mental and emotional attachment to them.

"Andy and I are going out for dinner, and you're welcome to join us for our first night out in Bar Harbor if you'd like to," Wella invited him as she prepared to leave.

"Thanks, but I think I've had my fair share of outings for one day," Logan declined her offer. "I'm going to enjoy the peace of being back home and sleeping in my own bed." He smiled. "I've been away from home for far too long."

Wella smiled. "At least see to it that you eat whatever delicious aroma from the kitchen that Cindy has the cook preparing for you."

"I will," Logan assured her, wrapping a towel around his waist and pulling on his shirt as he walked her to the front door. "I hope you and Andy enjoy your first night in Bar Harbor. Be sure to take a stroll down the boardwalk afterward."

"I will do that," Wella told him as she walked down the stairs to where her rental car was parked, turning to him before she climbed in. "I think you can take a break from sessions tomorrow, and we'll pick it up at the same time on Friday."

"That suits me," Logan said before saying goodbye and watching her pull out of the driveway.

Logan watched her car disappear, and once again he was alone with his thoughts. He needed to find a way to move past his anger and frustration to find a new path forward in his recovery. And perhaps, just perhaps, he needed to open himself up to the idea of therapy, of facing the demons that haunted him day and night.

He headed to his room to shower and prepare for dinner. As he walked into his room, he noticed a letter with his name on it propped against the mirror of his dresser. Logan walked up to it and picked it up, wondering who had left it there.

He opened it and pulled out a handwritten note.

Hi Logan

I don't know if you remember me, Bradley Danes. We went to school and played hockey together.

I was sorry to hear about what happened to you, and you have my utmost respect for what you were willing to risk for your country. I was glad to hear from your grandmother that you were recovering.

I know you've come home to finish your recovery and take it easy, but we need to talk. I have some information you may find helpful. A colleague of mine told me you were interested in finding out about your shadows.

I go for a run every morning around Central Lake. Meet me there tomorrow near the bridge at six a.m.

Bradley

His heart jolted at the mention of Central Lake. It was the lake in the woods behind Hope's bakery.

"If by shadows he means me being followed," Logan muttered. "How the heck would he know about that?" His eyes widened, and he pulled out his phone. "The only way he'd know about that is if he was following me and saw the men or if Annabell had told him."

Logan scrolled through his contacts and found Annabell's number to send her a message.

Did you tell Bradley Danes that I was being followed?

He didn't expect her to respond within a few minutes.

No, Bradley was the one who told me!

Logan's brows raised in surprise.

So much for not revealing your sources.

He watched as the dots started as soon as the message was read.

Bradley's not a source; he's a colleague and dear friend. I assume he reached out to you?

At least Logan knew Bradley wasn't part of the press trying to hound him for a story.

Yes.

Logan waited for her reply.

Good, listen to him and let him help you. He has a lot of contacts, and whatever you do, be careful.

Logan called an Uber to take him to his grandparent's store the following day. After being dropped at the store, Logan crossed the road, wondering where Hope was as he glanced at the bakery. Logan walked through the park and into the woods. He walked around the running path to the lake and froze as he neared the bridge.

"Hope?" Logan breathed, looking at her in surprise.

CHAPTER SEVEN

"Logan?" Hope looked at him and frowned. "What are you doing out here so early?"

"I was about to ask you the same thing," Logan threw her question back at her.

"I'm meeting someone," Hope told him, then asked again, "And you?"

"I am too....." Logan's voice trailed off as a thought struck him. "Are you here to meet Bradley?"

"How do you know that?" Hope's brow crinkled into a frown.

"Because I'm here to meet him too," Logan said, confused. "Do you know why he asked you to meet him?"

"He had a note delivered to me late yesterday to meet him at six a.m.," Hope said, pulling the letter from her pocket.

Logan walked closer and looked at the envelope. The handwriting was the same as on the envelope he'd received.

"I also got a letter from him," Logan explained. "They must've both been hand-delivered." He flipped the envelope over and looked at her. "Can I ask what he wanted to talk to you about that he asked you to meet him here?"

"If you tell me why he asked you to meet him here," Hope bargained.

"Sure." Logan nodded. "I think he may have information on the private security firm my parents have following me."

"Your parents are having you followed?" Hope's face crumpled in disbelief. "Do they think you're in danger?"

"It's a long story." Logan breathed and handed her Bradley's letter back. "What did he want to talk to you about?"

Hope had gone cold when Logan had told her his parents were having him followed. Could Logan's parents be having her followed too? Did they know something about Hope?

She decided to tell Logan the truth about why Bradley asked her to meet him here, "I noticed a blue sedan following me and watching me for a few days. I had someone I know run the plates, and it came back to be Bradley," Hope explained. "But before I could approach Bradley, he came to me and told me he thinks I'm being spied on."

"Spied on?" Logan looked at her in alarm. "Do you mean by being followed?" His brow knitted into a tight frown. "But why would you…." His eyes widened in realization, and Hope's heart stopped beating for a few seconds. "Maybe whoever's following me thinks we've been in touch again since…." His voice trailed off, and she saw emotion darken his eyes for a split second. "You being followed could be my fault."

"I'm not sure." Hope looked left and right along the jogging path for Bradley. He was ten minutes late. She looked at Logan, who was staring at her with a frown. "But Bradley doesn't just think I'm being followed. He thinks my car, business, and home are bugged."

"That's why he wanted to meet here," Logan guessed and nodded. "That makes sense." He ran his hand through his hair as he leaned heavily on his cane. "Bradley must think my place is bugged as well."

"He does seem to be a rather paranoid man." Hope gave a soft nervous laugh and glanced at her wristwatch. "Who is now nearly fifteen minutes late."

"Do you have his number?" Logan looked at her questioningly.

"No." Hope shook her head. "Would anyone be at the newspaper office this early?" She pulled out her phone. "Maybe they can give us his number?"

"I don't think they'll just hand it out," Logan said. "Maybe we should go there or to his house?" He rubbed his chin. "You wouldn't happen to know where he lives?"

"No, but your grandmother might!" Hope told him. "Bradley is engaged to Aida William's granddaughter."

"Tiffany?" Logan raised his eyebrows and gaped at her. "Champion figure skater Tiffany Williams?"

"Yes, and your grandparents went to Bradley's house for the engagement party," Hope blurted out without thinking and quickly added. "Your grandmother told me about it when I took Sydney around to her to train our dog, Barbie."

"My grandmother told me your daughter took one of the three puppies from Quiggly's last litter." Logan nodded, looked at his watch, and pulled out his phone. "My grandmother should be awake. I'll give her a call."

Hope watched Logan walk a few feet away from her as he called Lavinia. Her heart had been thudding in her chest like she'd run a marathon from the moment he'd called her name. Hope took a few quick breaths to steady her pulse and calm her frayed nerves. She didn't know if someone was actually following her. Or if they were if it was because of her liaison with the Hall family. Hope tried to reason with herself that it was no use panicking until she had all the facts.

"My grandmother gave me Bradley's address." Logan walked back toward Hope, pocketing his phone. "I can get a cab and go over there if you have things to do."

"Oh, I can drive us," Hope offered. "Wes is helping me out today and is opening the bakery."

"What about your daughter?" Logan asked, and she saw something flicker in his eyes but couldn't make out what it was. "Doesn't she have to get to school?"

"Sydney has a stomach bug," Hope told him. "She's staying with my mother for a few days because my brother wants me to cater for his Sunday barbecue."

"Oh, right." Logan's brows shot up. "Chase roped me into helping out with that as well." He looked at her sheepishly. "He asked me to help you out with anything such as a new grill, wood for the fire pit, smores ingredients, etcetera."

"Yes, he mentioned that," Hope said, feeling her cheeks heat as her mind instantly went back to the last time they'd planned an event together before giving herself a mental shake. "But I know you've just got home and want to take it easy." She gave him a tight smile. "So you don't have to worry about anything. Between myself and my bakery staff, we've got the barbecue covered."

"No, I want to help," Logan assured her. "It will be nice to do something normal again."

"Planning a function is normal to you?" Hope teased him as she started walking back toward the bakery.

"It's more normal than planning a rescue mission, spending hours in physiotherapy, or parading around at my mother's events," Logan told her as he followed.

"When you put it like that, I guess planning a barbecue is quite normal." Hope laughed as she let them into the back door to her apartment and the bakery kitchen. "Come in." She stepped aside for him to enter. "I'll get my keys, and we can go."

Logan nodded and followed her into the bakery kitchen and into her office.

"Wow." Logan gave a low whistle. "You've put a lot of work into the bakery since the last time I saw it."

"Yes, we've been expanding and upgrading," Hope told him, frowning when she noticed her desk calendar had been moved. She straightened it. "Marli and I can open our kitchens if we need to, as she now owns the building next door for her sweet shop."

"It's good to know you and Marli are still so close," Logan said, watching Hope get her keys and sweater.

"We have our moments," Hope gave him a smile as she led the way to the garage through the side door of the small hallway. "If you wait here, I'll get the car out of the garage."

She left him at the back door, opened the garage, and climbed into her car. Hope had reversed out and was waiting for Logan to climb into her car when someone called their names.

Logan turned and looked over his shoulder into the parking lot next to the bakery. It was Bradley.

"I guess he was running late," Logan said, sliding out of the car and closing the door.

Hope switched her engine off. She climbed out of her car and walked around the hood to where Logan was standing. They waited side by side as Bradley hurried over to them.

"Sorry, I'm late," Bradley panted after his dash across the parking lot, clutching a thick folder beneath his arm. He shook hands with Logan and exchanged a few pleasantries. "Are you okay with walking to the park bench near the duck pond?" He asked Logan.

"Of course." Logan nodded.

The three walked to the park bench, and Bradley asked Logan questions about his recovery and being back in Bar Harbor. Bradley sat in between Hope and Logan when they got to the bench. He looked around them before pulling the folder from beneath his arm. Hope began feeling like she was in a spy movie or having a bizarre dream and had to clear her throat to suppress a nervous giggle.

"Why are we here, Bradley?" Hope asked him, unable to wait to go through the thick file for answers.

"Because you and Logan are being tailed," Bradley told her, then looked at Logan. "I have asked Lance if he'd be so kind as to humor me and sweep both your homes, places of work, and vehicles for bugs."

"Really?" Hope looked at him in disbelief. "Unless a rival bakery and catering place is opening in town, why would anyone be interested in me?"

"I think you know the answer to that," Bradley's voice dropped, and he glanced at Logan, who had picked the first document in the file Bradley opened.

Alarm shot through Hope when she realized that Bradley must know about Sydney, and her eyes darted to the file on his lap.

"I thought Annabell said that Crow Security was following me?" Logan looked up from the document in his hand. "According to this document, the photos of me and...." He looked at Hope before continuing. "The photos she showed me were taken by a photographer from the Bar Harbor Daily."

"Reread the document," Bradley took the document and flipped it to the back page before handing it back to Logan. "Crow Security uses the photographer often when they need to work in and around Bar Harbor." He pointed to the page. "He was working for them when he was tailing you."

Hope watched Logan take out his phone and web search the photographer. "Oh, wow!" He whistled and turned his phone, so Hope and Bradley could see. "The photographer worked with a well-known war correspondent."

"Yup," Bradley confirmed, nodding. "So they know how to get a shot without anyone knowing." He flipped through the file and pulled out two larger envelopes giving one to each of them with their names on them. "You will find all the photos

I managed to pull from his system that he's taken of the two of you and your families over these past seven years."

"Seven years?" Hope choked, and her heart started pounding in fright. "No!" Her eyes widened as she stared at him in disbelief.

"I'm afraid so," Bradley's voice was low, and he gave her a tight smile before turning to Logan. "There are not many pictures of you, though, except from the few times you came home in the past seven years."

Hope's brows shot up as she leaned forward and caught Logan's eyes. "You've been back to Bar Harbor in the past seven years?"

"Yes, I breezed in and out quite a few times," Logan told her. "I asked my grandparents not to tell anyone, especially my parents." He flipped through the photos he'd taken from the envelope. "But judging by these photos, I think they knew."

Hope's mind reeled at that news, and she wondered why Lavinia or Rod had not told her about his visits or when it was that he'd visited.

Oh, no! Hope's hand went to massage the base of her throat nervously as thoughts raced through her mind. *Does he know about Sydney?* She glanced at him as he thoughtfully tapped the wad of photos on his palm. *Did Lavinia and Rod tell him?* She closed her eyes and gave herself a mental shake. *Stop it, Hope. You're being paranoid.*

"Why would my parents have me spied on every time I returned to Bar Harbor?" Logan's brows crinkled, and he looked questioningly at Bradley. "Do you know if they had me followed when I wasn't here?"

"As far as Annabell and I could find, there were only a few times Crow Security was commissioned to follow you when you were on leave from the Navy in California." Bradley pulled out another thinner envelope from the folder.

Logan's frown deepened as he went through the photos of

him in California. "I recognize some of these." He held one up of him at a function. "The last few were from the week before I went on my final mission for the Navy Seals."

Hope plucked up the courage to open the envelope Bradley had given her. Her eyes widened, and her heart jolted when the first few pictures were of her and Logan seven years ago. There were not as many as Hope thought there would be.

"I don't understand," Hope said to Bradley as she flipped through the pictures. "I thought you said I'd been followed for the past seven years?"

"You have been," Bradley confirmed.

"There are not that many pictures, and look," Hope showed him one. "This was taken when I was nine months pregnant with Sydney. It was the day I went into labor."

"Okay." Bradley looked at her curiously as she showed him the next one.

"This is a picture of me visiting Lavinia two years later." Hope showed him the following picture. "Then there are a few more of me a year later, and they are all of me going to the Hall's house." She flipped through a few more. "Or me going to the Hall's grocery store or shopping with Lavinia."

"So this is about me?" Logan looked at her, alarmed. "Hope is being spied on because of me?" He looked at Bradley for confirmation. "But why?"

"I'm sorry this may be a sensitive subject," Bradley said. "But it goes back seven years ago." He took the first pile of photos from Logan. "At the beginning of that summer, the pictures were all of you, Chase, and Rose."

"I was being followed at the beginning of Summer," Logan's eyes widened in realization. "Then when Hope and I —" He cleared his throat, and their eyes met as they leaned forward. "Crow Security started following you."

"That's what it looks like," Bradley told them. "Annabell and I have only been able to confirm a few of the instances over the past few years." He pulled out a few Crow Security documents to show them. "Look at these orders." He pointed to the page. "These instructions for March two years ago were to follow Hope Wright." Bradley showed them another similar document. "Look what they coincide with."

Logan took the two documents Bradley showed them, read them, and then his eyes sought Hope's. She'd seen what was on the papers before he'd taken them to get a closer look.

"A few days before Logan came to visit his grandparents in Bar Harbor, I would become a person of interest to Crow Security," Hope pointed out. "As well as while Logan was in Bar Harbor and then for a week after he'd left."

"Right!" Bradley nodded.

"I'm so sorry, Hope," Logan leaned forward and looked at her as he handed Bradley back the documents. "I didn't mean to drag you or your family, especially not your young daughter, into whatever my parents think they're achieving with this."

"You really think your parents are spying on you?" Hope looked at him, confused. "But why?" She shrugged. "Why would they need to spy on you?" It didn't make sense. "You're a grown man in the Navy, for goodness sake."

"I'm not sure," Logan said. "But you can bet I am going to find out!" He looked at the folder Bradley had. "Is all that about Hope and me?"

"No, not all of it," Bradley answered. "There is some stuff on some other people that Crow Security was following, and Annabell and I are looking into."

"Why do you have all that information on Crow Security?" Logan asked.

"Annabell has been researching them for a while now and pulled me in to help her a couple of years ago when I had a run-in with them," Bradley explained, looking at the folder. "We know what they are capable of, and so far, this is the only information we know they have on the two of you."

"So you started following me because Crow Security has been following me because Logan's back in town?" Hope's brows crinkled in disbelief.

"I'm sorry I scared you by following you, Hope," Bradley apologized. "But I was coming to see you early one morning two weeks ago, and when I got to the bakery, a teenager arrived at the same time I did, looking for you."

"What teenager?" Hope asked him.

"I don't know." Bradley shrugged. "But he knew who I was and that I would be there at that exact time. I knew the bakery would still be closed, but you'd be getting ready to take Sydney to school, and I was going to go around the back to find you."

"Why were you going to see Hope?" Logan looked at him questioningly.

"I got a tip that the vagrant burglar was casing out Hope's bakery," Bradley told him. "The tip mentioned that the vagrant had been seen sitting in the same spot for the past few days at the same time outside Hope's bakery." He opened the file again as he spoke. "Needless to say, the vagrant wasn't there when I arrived. So I thought I'd go see Hope and ask if she'd noticed the vagrant or anything suspicious in the past few days."

"What would a burglar want with my store?" Hope asked. "Have they got a sweet tooth?"

"I'm not sure," Bradley said. "The burglar has stolen mainly antiques in and around Bar Harbor over the past five months."

"Then they should've been staking out Marli's store, not mine," Hope said. "All I have is an old cash register and a few old baking tools."

"You're right," Bradley looked at her with interest before shaking his head. "Sorry, that's a different story." He gave them a tight smile. "Back to the letter story."

"Letter?" Hope looked at Bradley in surprise. "The teenager had a letter for me?"

Bradley dug in the file again and found a copy of the letter. "I kind of read it." He looked at her apologetically, handing it to her. "But I think I was meant to intercept it."

"You read and then took my mail?" Hope's eyes widened as she stared at him, ignoring the note in his hand.

"It wasn't technically mail. There was no stamp or postmark on it. Hope's name wasn't even on the envelope." Bradley pointed out. "I have the original locked away if you want to see it." Hope took the letter. "And like I just said, I think I was meant to get it." He pushed the letter toward Hope.

"Why would you be meant to get a letter addressed to Hope?" Logan stepped into the conversation.

"Because of the timing of the teenage boy getting there." Bradley turned to Logan as he pulled another document from the file. "The tip I'd gotten had told me to be at the bakery at that exact time to find the vagrant. The teenager delivering the letter told me the man said if the bakery was locked to give the note to me."

"Or so you say," Logan looked at Bradley accusingly. "You don't even know who this teenager is, so we cannot corroborate your story."

"I wasn't completely honest about knowing who the teenager was," Bradley admitted. "I did find out who he was, but only a few days after I took Hope's note." He lifted the file. "The same day, the teenager delivered a box containing all this information to my door."

"Why would someone send you all that information which I take is mostly about Crow Security?" Logan looked at him, confused.

"This isn't a letter!" Hope gasped as she read it. "It's a threat!"

"What?" Logan breathed, taking the letter from Hope and reading it aloud.

Don't think you're going to use your little secret to wiggle your way back into his life. If you go anywhere near him, I'll ensure your secret backfires on you!

Stay away from the Hall family!

Hope's heart jolted in her chest, and she felt as if someone was constricting her airway as breathing became difficult and panic surged through her.

CHAPTER EIGHT

"Hope!" Logan leaned forward and looked at her. "Are you okay?"

"No!" Hope shook her head. "I'm not okay." She swallowed, and Logan saw she was trying to be calm. "Someone threatened me."

"I knew this was my fault," Logan said again, through gritted teeth. "I'll sort this out with my parents. They're home next week."

"Your parents?" Hope looked at him, confused. "You think your parents are threatening me away from you and your family?" She reached over and took the copy of the note from Logan. "I don't know about that. This seems more—"

"Stalkerish?" Bradley finished for her. "When I started dating Tiffany, she'd just got back to Bar Harbor after that injury to her knee ended her career." He handed Hope the other letter in his hand. "And I got a similar letter to yours, Hope. It was also hand delivered by a teenager who'd been paid by some guy to deliver it."

"You were threatened about Tiffany?" Hope looked at him wide-eyed. "So you think this is a crazed fan of Tiffany and Logan doing this?"

"Or Tiffany and Melissa or Felicia," Bradley suggested. "If you compare the two letters, you'll see the handwriting is the same."

"When did you say the box of information was delivered to you?" Logan's brow creased thoughtfully.

Something about the timeline of the letter to Hope and Bradley getting the Crow security information nagged at him.

"About two weeks ago — a day or two after I intercepted the note for Hope," Bradley told him.

"Was that the reason Annabell agreed to do the interview with me?" Logan asked Bradley as the thought struck him. "Because I thought it was strange that she'd refused to interview any of the Hall family in the past. Then suddenly, two weeks ago, Annabell agreed to do my interview."

"That is something you'll have to ask Annabell," Bradley hedged and looked at his wristwatch, placing the file beneath his arm. "I'm going to have to run." He stood up and dug in his pants pocket, pulling out two business cards he handed them. "Let me know if you have questions or want to see anything else. But I will keep in touch with you and let you know when Lance can sweep the areas you frequent for bugs."

"I don't think that will be necessary," Hope said, looking overwhelmed. "I'm sure that's just a little extreme for whoever is doing this."

"I thought that too until I called Lance a few days after I got this file, and he accidentally came across a bug in my house," Bradley warned. "He did a sweep after that and found a few more."

"Oh!" Hope's eyes widened in surprise, and her heart pounded with shock. "What do you think, Logan?" She glanced at Logan for his opinion.

"I don't see how it can hurt." Logan shrugged and gave her a reassuring smile. "I'll speak to my grandparents and find out what I can about Crow Security."

"I was hoping you'd say that," Bradley told him. "I think you, more than any of us, will be able to gain access to the records we can't."

"Why would Logan be able to do that?" Hope gave him a curious look.

"Because my parents own the company!" Logan saw the look of shock resonate through her at the information he'd dropped on her. Then said defensively, "I didn't know we owned such a company until two weeks ago."

"I really have to go," Bradley said before Hope could say anything else. "Can I offer you a lift home?" He looked at Logan.

"Thank you." Logan accepted his offer. "That would be helpful."

"This is crazy!" Hope threw her hands up in the air. "And one of the reasons I hope my daughter never opts to get into show business, no matter how musically talented she is." She stood up and shook her head. "You don't get a moment of peace. Your face is plastered everywhere, so it's hard to disappear in a crowd. And your life is constantly on display for the world to see, and then there are the crazed fans."

"It's like living in a fish bowl where people are constantly tapping the glass," Logan explained, leaning on his cane to push himself off the bench and stand. "I feel that way all the time, and I live on the outskirts of all my parents' craziness."

They started making their way back to the bakery.

"I'm sorry I was late," Bradley said as they walked to the side entrance to Hope's store that was adjacent to the parking lot where Bradley had parked his car.

They were about to say goodbye when Hope stopped them by asking Bradley, "Oh, about the vagrant burglar." She looked questioningly at Bradley. "Is he real, and has he been sighted near my store?"

"He is, or rather they are, as we don't know if the burglar is male or female or working in a team or group," Bradley explained. "They've been breaking into houses, stores, warehouses, and—"

"Was it the vagrant burglar that broke into the local museum and stole that priceless artifact on loan from the London museum?" Hope's eyebrows raised up.

"Yes," Bradley said, nodding. "Or at least it was the burglar's MO." He sighed. "Like all the other burglaries. Other than a few sightings of the same vagrant outside the burgled places, there is not much to go on."

"So the burglar is a pro?" Logan gave a low whistle. "How many burglaries is the person suspected of?"

"Six in Bar Harbor in the last six months and quite a few more around Mount Desert Island," Bradley alarmed Logan and Hope by telling them.

"Why wasn't the public alerted to this?" Hope asked. "Most of us in Bar Harbor are quite lax regarding our security."

"I think the police didn't want to spread panic, and we did report it in the Bar Harbor Daily," Bradley pointed out. "But after the museum robbery, the burglar disappeared. We didn't hear about him until I got the tip about the vagrant being seen at your store."

"And since then?" Hope tilted her head.

"No, there have been no break-ins or sightings of the thief," Bradley assured her.

They said their goodbyes, and Bradley had just pulled away from the bakery parking lot when Logan asked him, "Why were you late for the meeting?"

"If I tell you, you can't tell Hope," Bradley glanced at him as he drove. "At least not yet."

"I can't promise that until I know what you are hiding from her," Logan told him. "She's my best friend's little sister and someone my grandparents are fond of, not to mention she has a daughter."

"I asked you both to meet at that park then so I could get

into the bakery, sweep it for bugs, and retrieve....." Bradley pointed to the glove compartment. "If you look in there, you'll see what I took from her desk that had been left there for her to find this morning."

Logan frowned and opened the glove compartment to see an envelope with Hope's name on it. "What is it with Bar Harbor and hand-delivered notes," he muttered, pulling the envelope from the compartment before closing it. "I feel like we're back in the eighteenth century when footmen delivered notes from door to door."

"Only no one can hack hand-delivered notes," Bradley pointed out.

"Only intercept them!" Logan looked at him accusingly before opening it and then nearly choking as he read aloud.

Back off from Logan, and don't even think about trying to pick up where you left off all those years ago. Because if you do, the secret you've been trying to keep will come out and not in a good way!

"You said this was on her desk in the bakery office?" Logan's brows raised up. "When?"

"Last night," Bradley told him. "But I wasn't quick enough to get it before her baker closed up."

"So when you nearly scared Hope to death, letting her know she was being followed, you were actually there to steal this?" Logan held the note up.

"Yes, and warn her," Bradley told him. "But by the time Hope left, the teenager had delivered the note to Wes, Hope's baker, when he couldn't find me."

"The teenager that delivered the first note and the files?" Logan asked.

"Yes," Bradley nodded. "He's the one that called me when he was contacted to deliver another note to the bakery."

"That was nice of him," Logan said sarcastically. "I bet his loyalty comes at a price?"

"He's a teenager trying to make some extra money, so yes, it does," Bradley confirmed. "But at least I get to know before more of those notes go out."

"More of these notes?" Logan's frown deepened. "Why do I get the feeling there is a lot to all this you haven't told me?"

"There is a lot I can't tell you because it's not my story or investigation," Bradley said. "I'm only part of it, and when I saw the handwriting on the first note to Hope, I knew we had the same enemy."

"A crazed fan of Tiffany and either Melissa or my mothers?" Logan added.

"I think so." Bradley nodded. "If you look in the folder on the back seat, you'll find more notes I've gotten from before my engagement to Tiffany."

"Wasn't she engaged to Hardy Bryant?" Logan remembered how Tiffany had ended things with the star quarterback and accused him of abuse. "I remember how that ended with her filing for a restraining order."

"Yes!" Bradley's eyes widened, and he shook his head. "That guy is one mean sucker."

"But his manager said that Tiffany was exaggerating and trying to ruin his reputation because of one small indiscretion," Logan turned and looked at Bradley. "Then, not long after the article came out, she had an accident and injured her knee so badly it ended her skating career."

"That's right." Logan saw Bradley's jaw clench. "Tiff is vague about the accident's details and insists that everything happened so fast. But she's sure she wasn't accidentally bumped into the path of the oncoming motorcycle. She was pushed."

"So you think she was scared into saying that?" Logan guessed.

"Yes," Bradley nodded. "The one thing that connects Tiff's accident to your's and Hope's case is that Hardy's security detail—"

"Is Crow Security," Logan finished for him.

"They were also Tiffany's security detail until she split with Hardy. The company decided he was the more lucrative client," Bradley's voice was laced with anger. "But get this." He glanced toward the backseat. "In the folder, you'll see pictures of Tiffany around Bar Harbor since she's gotten home."

"She's being spied on just like me?" Logan felt alarm zing through him. "So Crow Security following me and spying on me may not be my parents' work after all."

"We can't rule that out entirely," Bradley warned. "But unless your parents are obsessed with Tiffany, I doubt it."

"At least that puts my mind at ease to know they may not be the ones spying on me," Logan breathed as they pulled up to the gates of his grandparent's estate. Bradley rang the bell and told whoever answered it that he was dropping off Logan. The gates slid open. "Before I go." He turned and looked at Bradley. "You haven't finished telling me about breaking into the bakery to steal this note."

Logan returned the note to the envelope and left it in the compartment between the seats.

"While you and Hope were waiting at the lake, I broke in and lifted the note," Bradley told him. "Then went to my car, which I had parked a few blocks away from the bakery, and drove it to the parking lot where I met the two of you."

"We were on our way to your house to find you because we were worried," Logan told him. "Can you send me a copy of what you have in your file and the letters?"

"I can send everything that involves you and Hope," Bradley promised him.

“Fair enough,” Logan nodded and started to climb out of the car. “Keep in touch, and I’ll tell you what I find concerning Crow Security.” He closed the door and leaned in through the window. “If you’d give me the name of the teenager.”

“Please don’t spook him,” Bradley said. “He is a great contact, and whoever is sending these notes through Crow Security trusts him as they asked their security consultant to send it through him.”

“You failed to mention that Crow Security was commissioning the teenager to drop off the notes.” Logan’s eyes narrowed at Bradley. “Do you think whoever the security consultant is, he sent you the files too?”

“That was my thought, but the teenager doesn’t know who he is. All he can tell me about the man is that he’s a mountain with a military buzz cut. The man wears a stiff black suit, dark aviator glasses, and has a fox tattoo in a circle on the inside of his wrist.” Bradley told Logan.

“A fox inside a circle?” Logan’s skin prickled. “Have you had the tattoo sketched from the kid's memory?”

“No,” Bradley shook his head. “I’m a reporter, not an interrogator or a cop.”

Logan nodded, tapping the door as he stood straight, “I’ll see what I can find on my end.”

“Thank you, Logan,” Bradley leaned down to look at him. “And be careful.”

“You too,” Logan said and watched as Bradley drove away.

He was about to go inside when another car came up the drive. It was Wella. He turned and watched her park. Andy was with her, and they greeted each other as Wella ran up to him with a business card in her hand.

“I thought it was my day off from physio today?” Logan watched her suspiciously.

“It is, but I found a therapist for you in Bar Harbor,” Wella told him. “She came highly recommended.” She handed him the card. "Just in case you decide you want to sort out any mental block you might have that is holding your recovery back."

"You're not going to let up about this, are you?" Logan sighed, taking the card from her and looking at it with a frown. "Lucy James." His chin pulled in, and his frown deepened thoughtfully. "That name sounds awfully familiar."

"She knows your parents and your grandmother," Wella told him. "So maybe you know her through them."

"I guess." Logan shrugged before noting how smartly dressed Wella was. "You look nice."

"Yes, we're going to that new five-star restaurant in the next town over for brunch," Wella grinned. "It was Andy's idea."

"Enjoy," Logan said with a warm smile. "Let me know what the restaurant is like."

"I will," Wella walked to the driver's side of the car and slid in. She waved goodbye and pulled off.

Logan glanced at the card in his hand before stuffing it into his pants pocket and walking into the house while contemplating the benefits of going to therapy.

"Hello, Logan!" Melissa purred from the door of the front living room, nearly scaring him to death.

"Melissa!" Logan glared at her. "What are you doing here?"

"I realized what a shock you must've had yesterday seeing me here," Melissa told him. "So I thought I'd let you calm down and settle in, then come talk."

"About?" Logan gave a sigh as he looked at her wearily.

"Us, silly." Melissa gave a soft, throaty laugh. "Now that you're well on your way to recovery, don't you think it's time we put this crazy separation between us aside?"

"Why, after I've told you a million times," Logan said through gritted teeth. "Are you still assuming that our splitting up is only temporary?" He ran his hand through his hair in frustration. The woman just wouldn't take no for an answer. "I can't make this clearer for you, Melissa." He watched her eyes tear up but ignored it, knowing it was all an act. "We're through for good."

"You don't mean that!" Melissa's voice was soft and rough with emotion as she swiped a tear from her cheek. "I know you're only trying to protect me because of your injuries." She took a step toward him. "But you're better now." She smiled and touched his chest with both hands as she leaned closer. "Look at you. Soon you'll be walking without the cane as well."

Logan pulled her hands away and stepped back, dropping them before she got the wrong idea. His senses prickled from her implication that she was ready to get back with him because he was whole again.

"Melissa, I ended things long before I got injured," Logan reminded her. "And I really don't want to have this conversation with you again." His eyes narrowed as he tried to contain his anger. "I don't know what's going on in your life that makes you think I'll be able to fix it — *again*." He turned and started maneuvering her toward the front door. "But I'm tired of being your reputation clean-up crew, and I think it's time we both moved on to something real."

"And you think that little baker is real?" She stopped and spun around to face him, shocking him with the anger in her eyes and malice in her voice. "Your mother will never let that relationship happen."

"What?" Logan snapped.

"You heard me. And don't pretend you didn't know how your mother helped you get out of that mess with Chase's little sister all those years ago," Melissa sneered before her eyes widened in surprise at the look of shock on his face. "You actually didn't know." A cruel smile curved her lips. "Well, well. Isn't this a turn of events?"

"What are you talking about, Melissa?" Logan's eyes narrowed warningly, and his heart thudded in his chest.

"The little affair you had seven years ago," Mellisa surprised him by saying. "Oh, come on!" She laughed mockingly. "Did you really think for a minute your mother would let you marry a commoner like the little baker?"

"Commoner?" Logan's anger started to boil over as the shock at Melissa's words cleared.

"She's not one of us, Logan," Melissa drawled spitefully as she twirled her finger through her gold necklace.

He could see she was delighting in his shock and being able to goad him. He drew in a breath and forced himself to calm down.

"I think it's time for you to leave," Logan said in a low, controlled voice. "And don't come back here. You are no longer welcome in this house."

"That's not your call to make," Melissa lifted her chin and looked down her perfectly straight nose at him. "You *will* re-announce our engagement at your thirtieth birthday party, or your parents will not be pleased with you."

"I don't care if my parents are happy with my choices for *my* life or not, Melissa," Logan looked around and breathed a sigh of relief when he saw Cindy walking down the hallway. "It is *my* life, and I no longer have to dance to anyone else's tune." He waved at Cindy. "Cindy, would you mind seeing Melissa out?"

"Of course," Cindy smiled at Logan and walked toward him. "This way, Miss Shaw."

"Trust me." Melissa glared at Logan, ignoring Cindy. "You *will* do what I say." Her eyes narrowed. "Because if you don't!" She warned, her voice filling with venom. "You, your family, and your friends will all suffer the consequences."

With that, she rudely pushed Cindy out of her way, sending the smaller woman flying, before she spun on her heels and flounced out of the house. Logan lunged, ignoring the pain in his hip and leg, to grab Cindy as the front door was slammed shut, sending sound vibrations resonating through the entry hall.

"That woman is a snake, I'm sorry to say." Cindy stepped back out of Logan's grip. "I'm so happy that you are no longer with her."

"Cindy," Logan said, stopping her from walking away. "Do you know anything about my mother warning Hope away from...." He looked at the floor, not sure how to broach the subject. "Do you know anything about my mother being mean to Hope Wright, Chase's younger sister?"

"I know Hope," Cindy told him. "She brings her daughter Sydney here a few times a week." Logan's frown deepened as he noted Cindy fidget nervously. "Your grandfather gives her music lessons and helps her with her math homework. Your grandmother is helping her train her dog, and your grandparents are fond of Hope and Sydney."

Logan couldn't help but feel that it was rehearsed.

CHAPTER NINE

After Logan and Bradley left, a feeling of unease had settled over Hope. She had gone to her apartment and called her mother immediately to check on them. Although she missed Sydney like crazy, she was glad her daughter was staying at her mother's place for a few days. After having a shower, Hope made a mental note to contact Lance to come to sweep her building for bugs and cameras.

Whenever Hope thought about the meeting with Bradley and Logan earlier, she had to give herself a mental shake or a pinch to ensure she wasn't dreaming. Hope had done her level best to keep her daughter out of the spotlight that followed the Halls around. She had been nervous at first to let Lavinia and Rod into their lives, but Lavinia had been so supportive from the moment Sydney was born. She had to let them be part of Sydney's life.

They had been so good to Sydney and Hope over the past six years, and they had also been careful not to get Sydney caught in the pull of their or their family's fame. Hope appreciated how they had respected her wishes in that respect. As far as she knew, Lavinia and Rod had respected her wishes to keep Sydney's father a secret. At least until Hope was ready to disclose the truth — to Sydney and her father.

Something banged against the window, making Hope jump and yelp.

"Get a grip, Hope," she muttered, gripping her chest and feeling her heart beating wildly.

She had never been a nervous person, but after the conversation with Bradley this morning, she was jumping at her own shadow. Once dressed, she went downstairs to the bakery Wes had already opened and was busy baking.

"Good morning," Wes said cheerily as Hope entered the kitchen.

"Morning, Wes," Hope greeted him back, not feeling as happy as he was.

"Lance was here about twenty minutes ago," Wes told her. "He said he needed to speak to you urgently."

"Oh!" Hope's brows raised. "I'll call him after I've gotten some coffee."

"Brenda has a fresh pot of coffee in the shop," Wes surprised her by saying.

"Brenda?" Hope's brows knitted together. "Why is Brenda here?"

"I told her that Sally was off sick and how tightly we are stretched because of it at the moment," Wes grinned. "You know how she is."

"I appreciate it." Hope patted his thick muscular arm as she walked past him and into the front shop.

"Hope, honey," Brenda greeted her with open arms pulling Hope in for a hug. "How are you?"

"Much better now that you're here," Hope told her, walking over to the coffee maker.

Brenda and her husband, Wes Lovall, had worked for her parents at the Bakery for longer than Hope could remember. They were around the same age as her parents. Brenda had retired the year after Hope took over the bakery from her mother. Wes liked to think of himself as semi-retired, which meant he only worked a four-day week instead of a six-day one.

Hope was so glad to still have him with her. Although her new baker, Jane Iverson, was also excellent, she wasn't entirely on a par with Wes. Hope knew soon she'd have to hire at least two more people to help in the kitchen and one out front. As Hope's catering and event business grew, she relied increasingly on her bakery staff to carry out the day-to-day operations.

"Hope?" Brenda snapped her out of her thoughts. "Are you okay?"

"I'm fine," Hope said, sipping the coffee she'd just poured and nearly gagged when she realized she'd yet to put cream and sugar in it. "Oh, gross!"

"I was just bringing this to you." Brenda held up the cream jug and sugar pot. "But you were miles away."

"Sorry, I have a lot on my mind right now," Hope explained. "Sydney isn't feeling well, and Chase is coming home sometime today." She shook her head, holding out her mug while Brenda stirred in cream and sugar. "It's not as if I'm busy enough that my brother had to go and organize a Wright family barbecue he wants me to cater on Sunday."

"Yes, your mother invited us." Brenda put an arm around her shoulders. "Don't worry, love. You know Wes, and I will help you out."

"Thank you, Brenda," Hope said again. "I'm truly grateful that you came in to help today."

"It's not a problem at all," Brenda assured her. "Honestly, I was going to ask you if I could come back part-time." She smiled at the look on Hope's face. "I'm so bored at home during the day, and I've tried other hobbies, but I can't deny loving being in the shop or baking more."

"Brenda, if you're sure," Hope said, feeling relief flood her. "With the business expanding and growing as quickly as it is, I could use your help to manage it."

"Manager, eh?" Brenda grinned. "Are you offering me my old job back?"

"I am, part-time or full-time," Hope offered. "Right now, I could use whatever help I can get, and you know this bakery better than anyone."

"I would love that," Brenda told her.

"Oh, wonderful," Hope blew out a breath. "Welcome back, Brenda."

They hugged.

"Let me get through the morning rush, then why don't we meet for lunch, and you can go over the orders and delivery schedule with me," Brenda suggested. "I can see how I can help take some pressure off you. We can discuss some more staff, maybe." She glanced around the store as the morning customers started to pile in.

"Sounds like a plan," Hope said, looking at her wrist-watch. "I must go and make a call." She looked at the line. "Are you going to be okay?"

"Oh, this is nothing," Brenda assured her. "You go and do what you have to. I've got this."

Hope gave her a grateful smile and left Brenda to work the shop while she went back to her office. As she sat at her desk, her phone rang. She picked it up and saw it was Lance.

"Hello, Lance," Hope answered. "I was about to call you."

"Hi, Hope," Lance greeted her back. "You've been tough to get hold of today."

"Sorry, I've already had quite the day, and it's not even ten in the morning," Hope groaned. "Are you calling me to discuss Bradley Danes and his suspicions with me?"

"Do you have half an hour to meet?" Lance evaded her question.

"When?" Hope asked him.

"Now!" Lance said.

"I'm sure I can get away for a while." Hope's brows knit together, and little alarm bells went off in her head. "Where?"

"The place you fell off your bike and broke your arm," Lance said cryptically. "In ten minutes?"

"Okay," Hope said, glancing at the large clock on the wall over her office door. "I'm leaving now."

"Great." Lance went quiet for a few seconds before lowering his voice. "And, Hope, don't mention our meeting or where you're going to anyone."

The alarm bells in her head started to get louder, "Okay!"

Hope's hands were shaking when she hung up from Lance. Her unease started to subside when she saw Wes in the kitchen and Brenda in the shop. But now it was back and had brought its good friend's paranoia and fear.

Hope grabbed her car keys and left her phone and purse behind, giving a small laugh as she realized she had watched too many crime shows on television.

"Wes, I have to go out for a while," Hope told him as she walked out of her office and through the bakery toward the back door. "I'll be back in an hour, which should be more than enough time to get the bread delivery to the hotel."

"Not a problem," Wes said. "If you need me to, I can do the delivery. Just give me a call."

"Thanks, Wes," Hope called over her shoulder as she left the bakery.

As Hope backed out of the driveway, she put the stereo on and turned it up as loud as she could, hoping that if someone was listening to her, they would get an ear blast of static.

She headed toward the Windy Hills farm bike track where she'd had an accident on her bicycle when she was sixteen and broken her arm. Hope had been with her cousin Marli Rivers and her two older siblings, Cara and Simon. Lance had been

Cara's best friend and had joined them on the bike trail. There was also a BMX course at the farm, and as usual, Simon had to lead them astray and attempted the course. Their bikes were not designed for BMX, but Hope was still up for a good challenge and had done the course. She had flown over the first two jumps but failed to stick the landing on her third. Hope had fallen off her bike and broken her arm.

Ten minutes later, she was turning into the farm and pulled into a parking space. As she climbed out of her car, Lance pulled up beside her.

"Hi," Lance greeted her as he exited his vehicle. "That was good timing."

Hope and Lance got a coffee from the cafe and took it to one of the outside tables beneath the trees overlooking the lake.

"How long are you back in Bar Harbor for?" Hope asked Lance.

Lance sighed and leaned back in his chair, balancing his coffee in his hand, "I'm not sure." He lifted the cup to his lips and took a sip.

Hope watched his gaze move past her to the lake, and something in his expression made her think something was wrong with him or his job.

"Is everything alright, Lance?" Hope watched his head swivel toward her, and the look of surprise raised his brows. "You've not been yourself since you returned to Bar Harbor a week ago."

"That's very astute of you." Lance put his coffee cup on the table and leaned forward. "Between you and me—" He looked at her. "I'm actually on a leave of absence from the bureau right now."

That was news to her. Hope knew Lance loved his job at the bureau, and his mother had told hers that she had to beg Lance to come home for vacation as he was always so busy.

"Oh?" Hope's head tilted slightly to the side as she watched him intently. "I thought Lance Steel didn't take vacations." She pushed her hair back behind her ear as the breeze blew a few strands into her face. "The way your mother tells it, she has to coerce you into coming home for family functions. She planned to call the bureau to demand they give her son vacation time."

"My mother is prone to exaggeration." Lance laughed. "I've been working a case for the past two years, and a month ago, my partner was killed while we were chasing down one of the leads."

"I'm so sorry, Lance." Hope's face fell, and her heart filled with compassion for him.

"She died in my arms." Lance's eyes filled with emotion. "We'd been together since being at Quantico." He shook his head and drew in a breath. "I went a little overboard and might have crossed a line to find a witness."

"Ah!" Hope nodded in realization. "So, you were *asked* to take some time off to cool down."

"That's putting it kindly." Lance gave a self-mocking laugh. "Suspended pending investigation and further notice." He saluted with his coffee and took another sip.

A thought struck Hope, and her brow furrowed, "If you're suspended, how have you been helping Bradley with his investigation." Her eyes widened. "And how did you get the information I asked you to get for me?"

"I still have friends on the police force here in Bar Harbor and in the FBI," Lance told her. "Bradley got the Bar Harbor Daily to give me the position of temporary investigator for the paper, and I'm helping the police force with some consulting work."

"Wow!" Hope looked at him, impressed. "You've been suspended, and still, you're an overachiever."

"What do you mean by that?" He snorted.

"You can't even take it easy for five minutes," Hope

pointed out. "You've barely been home a week, and you've already got yourself two temporary jobs while waiting to get your permanent one back." She laughed and shook her head. "Cara is so right about you."

"And what does cool, sophisticated Cara have to say about me?" Lance asked, sarcasm dripping from his voice.

"What is it with the two of you these days?" Hope decided not to pursue that conversation path.

Although neither would talk about it, Marli and Hope had determined something had happened between Lance and Cara that had ripped their friendship apart. They had gone from being the best of friends to being unable to stand being in the same room together.

"We drifted apart," Lance told her, and she could see that he was not going to answer her question. "Some people do that."

It was more like they blew up their friendship bridge and created a vast ravine between them.

"Fine!" Hope sighed. "Should we move to the topic of why you asked to meet me out here in a cryptic way and warned me not to tell anyone where I was going?" She blew out a breath. "I feel like I've inadvertently stepped into a spy novel."

"Bradley asked me to sweep your building for bugs," Lance told her. "After hearing his story and finding out that he was following you, I decided to look into his investigation."

"Wait!" Hope held her palm up. "You just finished telling me that Bradley got you a position at the Bar Harbor Daily." Her eyes narrowed suspiciously. "Why wouldn't you have known that his sedan was following me?"

"Because it's not Bradley's car," Lance informed her. "It's Aida Williams' car." He ran a hand through his hair. "Bradley is using it because he feels it's safer than using his."

"He really has become paranoid!" Hope stated. "He told us about how he'd been threatened away from Tiffany."

"Men like Bradley don't usually become paranoid for nothing," Lance pointed out. "He's been on the front lines reporting on some war-torn countries in his career." He sat back and crossed his ankle over his knee. "So he's not easily spooked, but this case he's working on has him anxious and, as you pointed out, paranoid."

"That's why he's driving Aida's older model car," Hope guessed. "I don't think those models had GPS and can't be hacked."

"Yes." Lance nodded. "Exactly."

"Ever since I had that conversation with Bradley this morning, I've been anxious and a little nauseous," Hope admitted. "I must say, after your phone conversation where you basically warned me not to trust anyone—" She breathed. "I'm becoming paranoid. I didn't even bring my phone or purse with me just in case I was tracked through them somehow."

"You could be tracked through your phone, and someone could've put a device into your purse, but your car has GPS," Lance reminded her. "So if someone did want to locate you and they had the mean—"

"They could track my car," Hope finished for him. "Okay, so I was being dumb."

"No, not at all," Lance disagreed with her. "I think it was a sensible thing to do." He shrugged. "I don't have my phone on me either."

"So you do think someone is spying on me?" Hope accused.

"Hope, I don't want to alarm you," Lance said. "But this morning, while you were talking with Bradley and Logan, I got into your building and swept it."

"You did what?" Hope spluttered.

"I have a key to yours and Marli's buildings, remember?"

Lance held up his bunch of keys. "The two of you gave them to me in case of an emergency."

"I didn't even know you still had those," Hope hissed.

"Well, I do," Lance moved the conversation back to what he was telling her. "I didn't find anything in your apartment, but I did in your office."

"You did?" Hope choked, and her eyes widened as tiny zaps of shock zinged up her arm.

"Yes, and they were identical to the ones in Bradley's house," Lance told her. "I didn't tell Bradley I found anything. I told him the building was clean. Which it is now."

"Why didn't you tell him?" Hope looked at him curiously.

"Because they were planted by Tiffany's bodyguard," Lance's words alarmed her.

"I thought Tiffany no longer had private security?" Hope was confused. She was sure that was what Bradley had said. "Crow Security dropped her in favor of her ex-fiance."

"They did drop her as a client but not because of her ex-fiance," Lance told her. "Tiffany does still have a bodyguard. He is discreet, and neither Bradley nor her grandmother knows about him. They think he is her driver and assistant due to her inability to get around because of her *knee*."

"Why did you say knee like that?" Hope's eyes narrowed as she looked at him, and realization dawned on her. "You think she is exaggerating her injury?" She gave her head a little shake in disbelief. "But why would she do that? It basically ended her career."

"From what I've found out, it's not her knee that ended her career," Lance declared. "She was about to be disqualified from the world championships for tampering with two of her competition skates."

"That's absurd!" Hope shook her head in disbelief. "Tiffany is a regular at the bakery. I've seen her struggle with her knee and the brace she has to wear."

"I've seen her doctor's reports," Lance revealed. "There is

no reason for her to need all the therapy nor the brace she insists on wearing."

"I'm not going to ask how you got those reports." Hope held up both her hands. "But why would Tiffany or her mother have me spied on or my place bugged?" Her brow crinkled. "Why would either of them bug Bradley's place, for that matter?" Her frown deepened. "Do you think it's trust issues?"

"It seems Tiffany isn't as sweet as everyone thinks she is, just like her best friend." Lance reached into his jacket pocket and pulled out some photos. "These were taken two days ago."

"Is that Melissa Shaw with Tiffany at Stirlings Country Club?" Hope picked up the picture as alarm bells went off in her head again.

"It is," Lance confirmed. "Their bodyguards are also hired from the same new private security firm."

"I know that man standing near Melissa." Hope pointed to a large man dressed in a black suit with an earpiece and aviator sunglasses. "He's been Melissa's bodyguard for years."

"Crow Security didn't just drop Tiffany eleven months ago. They also dropped Melissa Shaw as a client," Lance informed her. "A month later, Melissa's longtime bodyguard who worked for Crow Security left them to join this new company."

"All that proves is the man is loyal to her," Hope stated. "But Lance, I don't follow celebrity gossip and like to avoid famous people." She reminded him. "So what has all this got to do with me? Why would any security company want to follow me?"

"Because you're not the only one that wants the secret you've been trying to keep all these years to stay secret!" Lance's words hit her like a tidal wave drenching her in shock and making her choke on the sting of it.

That's when the reality of her being spied on hit her. She

realized that her worst fears had been realized. More people than she knew had found out her secret. She was balancing on a knife edge of fear, dread, and having to do something she wasn't ready to do. It was time to let Sydney and her father know the truth. It was the only way she could see to end this terrifying invasion of her privacy.

CHAPTER TEN

Logan turned and wandered into the living room after finishing breakfast. He felt tired and worn out from a restless night and early morning meeting. Thinking of that meeting made his mind run through what Bradley had told them. Logan dropped into one of the armchairs and looked at the phone in his hand. Thinking about the morning meeting also made him think about Hope. In fact, the reason he'd had such a restless night was that his mind was filled with her. After their two meetings the previous day, Chase coaxed him into helping her with the Sunday barbecue.

It had all brought back memories of one of the best and worst summers of his life. Running into Hope again made him face the fact that he'd never gotten over that summer, and he'd only been fooling himself that he had. One of the main reasons he'd gone back to Melissa and stayed with her as long as he had was because she'd been the perfect buffer. Melissa was not a threat to his heart, and because their relationship was a smoke screen, it kept him safe from having his heart broken again. Or having to try to move on when he knew he never really would.

Sounds of heavy footsteps coming towards him quickly caught his attention. Logan turned as Maverick and Quigley barreled toward him excitedly. Their bodies twisted as their tails zipped back and forth as they pranced around him, vying for his attention.

"Hey, you two," Logan laughed, rubbing their heads, and that's when he noticed all the pictures in the back part of the room near his grandfather's grand piano.

He stopped patting the dogs and pushed himself out of the chair, ignoring his agonized hip as it protested with burning pain. Logan hobbled towards the shelving next to the grand piano at the far side of the room. His eyes widened when he saw all the pictures of who he figured was Hope's daughter from a small baby to a more recent picture with her dog.

Logan was about to pick the one up with Lavinia, Sydney, Rod, and the puppy when he heard the front door open and his grandmother calling him. Before Logan could turn and walk toward the front of the house, the dogs started to bark excitedly, giving away where he was.

"There you are!" Lavinia all but sang as she rushed forward with her arms extended to hug him. "It's so good to have you home." She kissed his cheek.

"Hey, kid," Rod greeted Logan with a hug. "We're sorry we couldn't be here when you got home yesterday." He patted his chest. "Had to go get the old ticker checked out."

"It's fine, I understand," Logan assured them. "How is everything with your heart, Grandad?"

"I'm fit as can be," Rod smiled and looked at his watch. "Oh shoot, I'd better get going if I'm going to make the bowls tournament."

"Okay, dear," Lavinia said as he pecked her cheek. "Remember to put on sunscreen and wear a hat."

"Always," Rod said, rushing out the living room door with

two Cane Corsos following him in hopes it was to take them for a walk.

"Grandmother," Logan looked at the shelf. "Are those pictures of Hope's daughter, Sydney?" He pointed to them. "There's an awful lot of them."

"Why, yes!" Lavinia said, turning towards the wall. "Beautiful isn't she?"

He noticed something flicker in his grandmother's eyes before she answered him. Logan couldn't be sure, but it looked like a moment of — fear.

"Do you know I've known Sydney from the moment she was born?" Lavinia told him proudly, and he watched her eyes fill with love as she reached out and ran her hand over a baby picture of Sydney. "Hope was making a delivery here the day she went into labor on the house's front steps."

A memory flashed through Logan's mind of him leaving to return to the Navy and bumping into a highly pregnant Hope on the doorstep. A frown marred his brow as a thought struck him like an arrow through the heart, crushing his soul as his breathing became difficult. He sat down on the piano stool, gripping the corner of the instrument to steady himself and forcing air into his lungs as his mind whirled.

Lavinia's hand went to her throat while keeping her eyes on the photos. "I rushed Hope to the hospital." She started twirling her necklace, lost in her memory of that day and oblivious to how her story affected Logan. "I called Clair, but she was out of town at a book signing. She did her best to return to Bar Harbor as soon as possible, but by then, little Sydney had already come into the world." She smiled at the memory. "I had been with Hope all day through the entire thing."

Lavinia picked up a photo of newborn Sydney.

"Was that the day I left to return to the Seals?" Logan said through gritted teeth.

Lavinia turned to look at him, and a frown knitted her

brow. "You know, I think it was." She gave the photo one last look before putting it back on the shelf in its place of pride.

Logan's chest felt like it was on fire and he could hardly breathe as he finally let the truth that had been staring him in the face for the past seven years in. "Who is Sydney's father, Grandmother?"

Logan saw the emotion flitter in his grandmother's eyes before she answered, "Sweetheart." Her voice was stern. "You know that's not for me to gossip about, and something only Hope can tell you."

"Don't you know?" Logan pressed. "Or are you hiding the truth for her?" His eyes narrowed. "Is Hope ashamed of who the father is?" He felt his anger start to rise. "Or maybe she doesn't know who the father is?"

"Logan!" Lavinia looked at him warningly, her eyes flashing with anger. "What a terrible thing to say." Her eyes narrowed and her shoulders stiffened. "I'm sorry, but this is not a topic up for discussion. Not with me anyway." She shook her head, not taking her flashing eyes off him. "I can't believe you of all people could be so nasty."

"What's the big deal about telling people who Sydney's father is?" Logan knew he was being unreasonable and insulted both Hope and his grandmother, but something inside him was driving him.

"Hope *does* know who Sydney's father is," Lavinia hissed. "She is also very protective over her daughter and with good reason." Her eyes bore into him. "I don't ever want to hear you say anything like that about Hope ever again. While I'd expect something like this from your diva mother, I'd never expected it from you."

Logan and Lavinia stood staring at each other both seething for a few seconds before Cindy walked into the room, breaking the ice that was forming around them.

"I thought I heard you come in," Cindy greeted Lavinia. "Can I get you a pot of tea?"

"Hello, Cindy," Lavinia gave Logan one more icy glance before smiling at their housekeeper. "I would love a pot of decent tea." She smiled. "You'd think a five star hotel could serve a decent pot of tea? But no!" She threw her hands up dramatically. "I've been dying for a pot of yours."

She looked at Logan asking stiffly, "Will you join me?"

"I have a few things to do," Logan declined the invitation. "Chase wants me to pick up a grill for his mother."

"Oh, yes, the Sunday barbecue," Lavinia remembered with a curt nod. "Call Winston if you need a ride into town."

Winston was their butler, chauffeur, and estate manager. He and Logan's father, Stan, grew up together as Winston's father had been Rod's estate manager. Between Winston and Cindy, they kept Hall Manor running like a well-oiled machine.

"I'll do that," Logan told her.

With that, she gave him one more cold glance before she turned and followed Cindy out of the room. Logan looked at the pictures of Sydney once again and decided it was time he had a serious talk with Hope, and the sooner the better. He had to know once and for all who Sydney's father was and why his grandparents would keep pictures of Sydney all over their home. Because to him there could be only one reasonable explanation for that which would mean a whole lot of people had been lying to him for over six years.

He was about to call her when he decided it would be better not to give her an excuse not to meet him or tip her off about what he wanted to talk about. Logan's best option would be to pay Hope an unexpected visit and catch her off guard. He slid his phone into the pocket of his jeans and went to find Winston. Today would be a perfect time to shop for a grill and some bits for Chase's barbecue on Sunday. Because Logan knew Sydney was with her grandmother— it was the perfect day to have a serious conversation with Hope about her.

Twenty minutes later Winston dropped Logan off at his grandparent's store. His first stop was to get a grill and the items he promised Chase he'd organize for the barbecue. That took him a good twenty minutes and by the time he crossed the road toward Hope's bakery Logan was calm. Although he still hadn't a clue how he was going to broach the subject he wanted to discuss with her.

He walked around to the side door of the bakery where he found her coming out of her garage.

"Hope?" Logan called, startling her.

"Logan!" Hope hissed, her hand going to her throat. "Good grief, you scared me."

"Sorry." Logan apologized. "I didn't mean to."

"It's not your fault." Hope sighed, holding up her hand. "It's been a crazy day, and it's only just past lunchtime."

"I know what you mean," Logan sympathized with her.

"I guess our early morning meeting set the tone for both of our days today." She gave a small laugh.

He nodded in agreement before stepping closer to her and asking, "I was wondering if you had some time to talk."

Logan saw a moment of panic flash in her eyes before her shoulders stiffened slightly.

"Sure." Hope frowned and gave him a curious look. "Do you have information about Crow Security?"

His eyes caught something taped to the door, "Is that a note?" Logan pointed to the door before answering her question.

Hope turned and pulled it from the door, reading aloud.

We dropped Barbie off for a few hours while Sydney and I went shopping. Mom.

"Who's Barbie?" Logan asked as he watched her roll her eyes and shake her head.

"Sydney's puppy," Hope told him, pushing the door open carefully. "Just be careful. She's not too good around strangers."

"Is she the dog from my grandmother?" Logan followed Hope inside, closing the door behind him.

"Yes," Hope confirmed. "She's eight months old and still learning manners."

Logan saw Hope stop in the small entryway, her frown deepening as she listened tentatively.

"Is something wrong?" Logan lowered his voice worriedly.

"It's far too quiet," Hope told him, moving toward the back room that led into her back garden, where she froze. "Oh no!"

"What?" Logan stepped up behind her.

His heart jolted, and his pulse raced as he was close enough to her that her scent teased his senses. Logan clenched his jaw and balled his hand into a fist to control his wayward thoughts.

"The back gate's open!" Hope hissed before being spurred into action.

Logan watched as she grabbed the harness and leash from the wall next to the small room before rushing out the back door and through the garden gate to the park. He followed her as fast as he could with his limited range of motion and reliance on a cane.

"Barbie!" Hope called as she dashed toward the duck pond, and he noticed the big black dog chasing after some birds.

Logan got to the pond where Hope was standing and got the harness on Barbie. She had just attached the leash to Barbie's harness when a flock of geese landed near them. Logan saw what was going to happen before it did. He tried to reach out to grab Hope, but by the time he got close enough to catch her, Barbie had taken off after the birds. The big dog knocked Hope flying into the pond in her haste to chase her feathered friends.

The loud shriek, followed by a splash, echoed through the park, which luckily was empty except for the three of them and some birds. So no one that could talk saw Hope's unsolicited dip into the pond. Logan quelled the urge to laugh especially seeing the black look on Hope's face and stepped forward to offer her a hand up.

"I'm sorry, Hope, I tried to grab you," Logan swallowed down the laughter as he pulled her out of the pond.

Her hair was plastered to her face, and her clothes were soaked through, clinging to her lithe figure, making her shiver as the cool breeze wafted over them.

"Here." Logan slid his light jacket off and put it over her shoulders, getting an instant sense of déjà vu as his mind flashed back seven years ago to the first time they kissed.

"Thank you." Hope pulled it around her. "You would think I'd have learned by now not to harness Barbie next to a body of water." She picked the leash she hadn't managed to fasten off the ground. "Barbi!e" She snapped, making the big dog stop in her tracks. "Sit!"

Hope held up her hand, and Barbie did what she was told, waiting patiently for Hope to catch up to her.

"So that's how it's done," he heard Hope say, and his heart jolted when she turned to look at him with a grin. "Your grandmother was right. I need to put more authority in my voice commands."

Logan stayed back, trying to catch his churning emotions as he watched her secure the leash and get Barbie to walk steadily at her side.

"Promise you won't tell your grandmother that this happened again," Hope stopped in front of him, snuggling into his jacket.

"You have my word," Logan promised and couldn't help

the smile that twitched his lips. "How many times has this happened?"

Logan walked next to Hope and Barbie back to the bakery.

"Too many times to admit to without me wanting the ground to open up and swallow me from embarrassment," Hope told him. "I need to take a hot shower and wash the pond scum off me."

Hope led them inside the gate, which she closed and locked behind them before taking off Barbie's harness. The dog shot off inside and up the stairs to Hope's apartment.

"I could put the kettle on and make us a cup of coffee?" Logan offered. "While you have a shower."

"That would be great." Hope started walking up the stairs.

Barbie was waiting patiently by the closed door, which Hope opened for them to enter.

"The apartment looks a lot different from when Chase and Thorn lived here." Logan noticed how nice and modern it was but still had a warm, homey feel.

"Yes, I remember my older brothers' bachelor pad." Hope stood next to him in the living room and slipped out of his jacket. Her eyes widened with dismay noticing it was damp. "Oh, it's all wet with pond scum."

"That's okay," Logan assured her, reaching out to take it and feeling a zap of emotion zinging up his arm when their fingers brushed in the exchange. "Cindy will get it dry-cleaned."

"Oh, no. I can get it cleaned for you," Hope told him.

"No, seriously, it's okay." Logan put the garment on the small round table in the corner of the room and noticed a pretty pink hair brush with a princess on it. "Yours?" he teased, pointing to it.

"Sydney went through a princess phase last year," Hope told him. "She has a wardrobe full of princess outfits my mother and your grandmother made for her."

"My grandparents are very fond of Sydney," Logan said softly, his eyes dropping to the brush.

"Sydney is just as fond of them," Hope told him, shivering.

"You're cold, you should shower, and I'll put the kettle on." Logan gave her a tight smile.

"You know where the kitchen is." Hope smiled at him gratefully before walking out of the room and heading toward her bedroom, calling over her shoulder. "I won't be long. Make yourself at home."

Logan watched her close her bedroom door at the end of the hallway before going to the kitchen. He had put the kettle on the stove and found the mugs and coffee. He opened a drawer looking for the spoons but found it had documents, folders, and bits in it. The top folder was labeled:

Sydney L. Wright Personal Details and Medical History

Logan stared at the folder for a few seconds, his heartbeat picking up speed. He looked toward the kitchen door and stood listening. He could still hear the hiss of the water system from the shower. Logan reached into the drawer. His hand shook as he pushed the folder open. A feeling of guilt mixed with trepidation washed over him at snooping through Hope's things but he couldn't stop himself. Logan had to know and he was sure there would be answers in the file that he desperately needed to know.

He was content that he could still hear the water sloshing through the pipes as he rifled through the neatly filed papers. Logan's stomach knotted when he came across Sydney's birth certificate. But his excitement soon turned into disappointment when he found no father listed on the document. Logan slipped the document back into the folder and saw Sydney's medical records. A frown creased his brow as he read that Sydney had a rare blood type.

Logan's pulse rate increased and his eyes widened when he saw what it was. His heart thudded against his rib cage making his body vibrate with shock as his nerve endings tingled. There were only three other people in Bar Harbor or in the State of Maine with RH Null blood and he knew that because he was one of those three. The other two were his grandfather and father. His throat went dry and his head started to ache, making him realize how tightly he'd clenched his jaw. Logan may not be a scientist or lab technician but he did know that he'd inherited his blood type from his father. So he was pretty sure Sydney would've done the same and unless Hope or someone in her family was RH Null, Logan had his answer.

A low groaning noise from the kitchen pipes pulled him from his thoughts as he heard the shower turn off. Logan quickly stuffed the medical record back into the file, his eye stopping on Sydney's birth certificate again, and his breath caught as he read her middle name. Tears sprang to his eyes, and a burning sensation started in his throat as his heart thudded painfully as he shut the drawer. Logan knew he needed concrete proof that he was Sydney's father because he now knew that his grandparents and maybe even his best friends had been lying to him all this time. Logan doubted he'd get a straight answer from them. And if Hope had kept this a secret from him for this long she was probably never planning on telling him.

The kettle whistled, making him jump, and he pulled it off the stove, noting how his hands shook. Along with the myriad of questions tumbling through his mind, Logan was knocked by waves of emotion. Varying from shock to anger, to astonishment, back to anger, and the one he was trying not to acknowledge was the one cutting off his air supply — regret.

Suddenly Logan couldn't face Hope. Not now. He needed to clear his head and figure things out. Logan also needed someone to find something to get proof of who Sydney's father was. He remembered Sydney's princess brush on the table in Hope's living room. Logan walked as quickly as he could with the blasted cane to the living room. He glanced at Hope's bedroom door before silently slipping into the living room and pulling as much hair as he could from the hairbrush. He picked up his jacket and slipped the hair into the inside pocket. Logan walked to the living room door when he heard a soft bark and turned to see Barbie lying on her bed watching him accusingly. Guilt washed over him again.

"Don't judge me!" Logan hissed at the dog. "This is the only way."

Barbie gave another soft bark before whining and resting her large head on her paws making him feel even more guilty as he heard Hope's bedroom door opening.

Shoot! He was hoping to have slipped away before seeing her.

"There you are," Hope said, catching him leaving the living room and frowning when she saw his jacket hooked over his arm. "Is everything okay?"

Her hair was damp from the shower, and she smelled of wild blossoms and spring. Logan gave himself a mental shake, forcing himself to concentrate on what he had to do.

"I have to go," Logan lied, unable to stop his clipped tones. He cleared his throat. "I got a call, and there is something I must deal with urgently."

"Oh!" Hope said, sounding a little disappointed, which made his traitorous heart do a little flip in his chest. "Okay, I hope it's nothing serious." She gave him a tight smile.

"No, it's just something I must take care of immediately. I nearly forgot about it with everything that happened this morning with Bradley," Logan found himself lying again.

Logan started walking toward the door with Hope following him.

"Do you need a ride?" Hope asked him.

"No, Winston will take me," Logan assured her, pulling out his phone and using his app. to get a cab as they walked down the stairs to the bakery.

Logan said goodbye and rushed across the street to his grandparent's grocery store to wait for his taxi. It didn't take long, and it pulled up.

"Where to?" the cab driver asked him.

"The hospital," Logan said, climbing into the back of the vehicle, wondering if a lab technician he went to school with still worked there.

"Are you okay?" The cab driver asked him.

"I'm not sure!" Logan answered honestly. "And as soon as I get some results back." He patted his jacket pocket where the hair was. "I'm not sure I'll ever be again."

CHAPTER ELEVEN

Hope was confused by the sudden change in Logan. There was a touch of awkwardness between them. But they were doing their best to ignore it and were getting along. Even though Logan had tried his best to conceal it, Hope had felt the sudden change in him. So what had happened in those ten minutes while she had showered?

Hope shook off the feeling of déjà vu she got remembering the last time he'd gone cold and distant on her. Her heart thudded, knocking on the scar their previous encounter had left on her heart seven years ago.

"Hope," Jane Iverson, Hope's second baker who was also a top chef, called her.

Hope turned away from staring at the empty doorway where Logan had exited and turned to look at Jane standing in the bakery doorway.

"Hi, Jane," Hope greeted her. "Is everything okay?"

"I was going to ask you the same thing." Jane looked pointed toward the open door as Hope pushed it closed.

"I'm fine," Hope assured her with a smile. "I've just got a

lot on my mind with all the new events we've got to cater for and my brother adding a Sunday barbecue to my diary."

"Yes, he sent out the invites, and I was going to ask if you needed us to make some pastries and hors d'oeuvres for it," Jane said.

"I was about to put a list together," Hope told her. "And I would, as usual, love your input."

Hope had hired Jane to help her with the catering and bakery side.

"Of course," Jane agreed with a nod. "Brenda asked me to let you know that she wants to take a late lunch break and asked if you wouldn't help out in the front."

"Yes, I can do that." Hope looked at her wristwatch, surprised to see what the time was. "Can you stay behind for half an hour or so this evening so we can put a quick menu together for Sunday?"

"Sure." Jane nodded, stepping aside so Hope could walk into the bakery as one of the oven alarms went off. "Oh, I'd better get the ginger snaps from the oven."

"I'll get more kitchen staff soon," Hope promised, breezing through the kitchen. "I have three potential hires to interview tomorrow."

"That would be a great help," Jane said, picking up the tool to take the baking trays from the oven.

Hope walked into the front store where Brenda was serving a customer.

"Hey, I'm here," Hope called, stepping beside her. "You go take your break."

"I was going to grab a coffee and sandwich, then come talk to you about the bakery," Brenda said, using some hand sanitizer from the counter.

"You've been on your feet the entire morning," Hope pointed out. "Why don't you rather relax in my office and jot down your ideas." She put on one of the clean aprons from behind the counter. "I've asked Jane to stay on a bit later today if you could do the same."

"Okay," Brenda agreed. "That sounds like a much better plan."

"Can I be forward and ask you to go over the orders for next week while you're relaxing," Hope pulled an *I'm sorry, but please, please* face.

"I was going to do that anyway," Brenda admitted. "I can see how swamped you are, child." She patted Hope affectionately on the arm before going to the espresso machine and making them both a quick vanilla latte. "I'll be back in an hour if you're okay for that long?"

"Of course," Hope assured her.

Brenda had been gone for fifteen minutes, and Hope was handling the few customers wandering into the store when her heart jolted and froze in her chest. Hope's breath caught in her throat as a large bald man in a black suit with aviator sunglasses entered her shop.

"Hello," the man's soft clipped tones seemed to echo through her ears and make her heart beat faster than it already was.

Hope's mind flashed back to the conversations she'd had with Bradley, Logan, and Lance that day. Hope flinched when she saw him reach into his suit jacket, and she hadn't realized she was holding her breath until she noticed him pulling out a note. Hope had to stop herself from sighing with relief and then try to act as normal as possible.

"Can I help you?" Hope forced herself not to stammer.

"Yes, my employer would like these pastries and pies, please," the man's voice softened as he handed her the note.

Hope took it out, noticing the man had a tattoo on his wrist as his sleeve rode up on his arm. She couldn't remember if Bradley had said that the man who'd given the notes and files to the teenager had a tattoo, but she was pretty sure he'd said bald and giant. The man was bald, extremely tall, and dressed like the teenager had described to Bradley.

Hope made a mental note of the tattoo, trying not to stare at him. She gave the man a tight smile and opened the message, nearly dropping it when she recognized the handwriting. It was the same as the threatening note to her that Bradley had intercepted from the teenager. Hope needed to somehow make a copy of the note. She read the list and looked up at him.

"I think we have some of the chicken pies fresh from the oven," Hope told him, giving him as warm a smile as possible. "Can you give me a minute to go and get them?"

"Not a problem," the man said, making Hope feel nervous not being able to see his eyes through those dark glasses.

"Why don't you help yourself to a complimentary coffee and take a seat while you wait?" Hope pointed to the corner cabinet at the far end of the bakery near the tables and booths.

The man nodded, turned, and walked to the coffee pot. Hope breathed a sigh of relief before dashing into the bakery and through to the small room that housed various kitchen, shop, and office supplies. It was also where the printer and copier were. Hope quickly made a copy of the note and nearly knocked Jane down as she rushed out of the room.

"Whoa!" Jane said, wiping her hands on some paper towel. "Where's the fire?"

Hope shoved the copied note into her pants pocket and handed the one the man had given her to Jane.

"Do you have any freshly baked pies and pastries on this list?" She looked at Jane hopefully.

"As a matter of fact, I do," Jane said with a smile, taking the note and walking to the cooling racks. "I see you've gotten Mrs. Williams's Thursday order?"

Hope froze as Jane's words sank in, "Did you say, Mrs.

Williams?" Her eyes widened in realization. "Not Tiffany Williams?"

"No, not Tiffany." Jane laughed. "I doubt Tiffany would eat anything on this list. Too much sugar, carbs, and fat."

"So Aida Williams wrote that list?" Hope was dumbfounded. *Aida Williams?*

"Oh, no, not Aida Williams, Gloria Williams," Jane corrected. "Gloria takes these treats to the retirement village where Aida lives. Every Monday, Mrs. Williams gets an order for the resident's quilting club and an order for their book club on a Thursday."

Hope felt her eyeballs start to dry out, her eyes were so wide with shock.

"Are you okay?" Jane asked her worriedly, then blinked when something dawned on her. "Oh, if you're worried that we don't have enough to fill the order. I have it under control. Mrs. Williams comes to the bakery around the same time on those two days. So Wes and I always have her orders ready and waiting."

"What?" Hope realized she was staring and gave herself a mental shake. "Oh, no, I'm not worried. I'm just—" Her mind scrambled for an excuse. "Just surprised that Gloria Williams used my bakery when she used to go to one out of town."

It wasn't exactly a lie. Gloria Williams and Hope's mother, Clair, didn't get along; they had a falling out many years ago.

"Oh, no, Mrs. Williams, her mother-in-law, and even Tiffany are here at least two to three times a week," Jane told her. "They love your bakery."

"Thanks to you and Wes." Hope gave a nervous laugh. "Did you say that Mrs. Williams usually collects the order herself?"

"Yes," Jane nodded as she reviewed the list and gathered the items. "Why?" She stopped what she was doing to look curiously at Hope.

"Oh, no, it's just a man who came in to collect it today,"

Hope told her. "He looks like a bodyguard dressed in a stiff black suit and dark aviators."

"Oh, that must be James Grant," Jane told her. "He has come in here a few times but usually to help Tiffany as her driver. I have a suspicion, bodyguard, as well."

"Oh!" Hope's eyebrows shot up. "You know quite a lot about the Williams family."

"Yes, Tiffany and I go way back," Jane explained. "We were at school together, and believe it or not." She gave a nervous laugh. "Skating competitors until I blew my ankle out."

"I did not know that," Hope said. "Chef and baker is a far cry from champion figure skater."

"Phffff!" Jane waved her hand in front of her. "I wasn't really going to go places with figure skating. It's too much hard work."

Hope's brow creased, "Do you know if Tiffany is friends with Melissa Shaw?"

"You mean actress and pop star Melissa Shaw?" Jane popped a pie into a pastry box and nodded. "Yes, I believe so. Back in high school, Tiffany loved to brag about how her parents and Melissa's parents were such good friends."

"I thought Tiffany was a nice sweet girl, not one who liked to brag." Hope's frown tightened.

"Oh, she has her sweet moments," Jane emphasized with the spatula, her eyes darkening with a flash of anger. "But, trust me, she's not someone you want to get in the way of." She shook her head and put some cupcakes into a box, giving a snort. "Her mother can be just as bad as Tiffany, though." She widened her eyes and pulled in her chin while something Hope couldn't grasp flashed in her eyes. "I remember how that woman pushed Tiffany at our junior skating competitions. It was always the coach's fault if Tiff didn't win for some reason." She put her hand on her hip. "I remember this one competition where Mrs. Williams accused one of the other mothers of tampering with Tiffany's ice skates."

"Oh, they always seem so nice when I've bumped into the family," Hope told her.

"Yes, until you cross them or something goes wrong," Jane's voice dropped, as did her eyes for a few seconds before she looked at Hope, her smile back on her face as the service bell in the shop rang. "You go tend to the customers. I'll bring this order through when I'm done."

"Thank you, Jane," Hope thanked her and walked through to the shop.

Her mind was reeling with Jane's information about the Williams family, especially over the realization that Tiffany's mother may have written the threatening letter to Hope. It didn't make sense to Hope why Tiffany's mother would send her threatening letters or have Hope spied on.

As she served the customers in the shop, Hope's eyes kept sliding to the man sitting casually in a booth, watching people walk by and sipping a cup of coffee. According to Jane, his name was James Grant, and Hope made a mental note of it, wondering if Lance knew who the man was. When Brenda took over the shop, Hope would call Lance and tell him what she'd found out. Although he probably already knew, Hope didn't know who else to trust with the information.

She glanced to the left wall of her shop, which was joined to Marli's sweet shop, wishing that her cousin was back from a course in something to do with making chocolates. Hope missed Marli and her daughter, who was staying with Marli's older sister, Cara. She needed Marli's calm and bright ideas because if she was honest with herself, Hope would admit to holding on with every last ounce of willpower she had to stop herself from spinning out. The past two days felt like Hope had been caught in an avalanche of emotions while getting caught in the crosshairs of a crazed stalker.

Hope raised her eyebrows at the thought of the crazed

stalker, who may just be the mother of a sports star which was absolutely bizarre!

How on earth did I get tangled in this mess? Hope couldn't believe after trying all these years to skirt the sidelines around the famous people in Bar Harbor, she'd been pulled into what she thought of as showbiz craziness.

"Hope?" Jane's voice pulled her from her thoughts. "Here's the order for Mrs. Williams."

Jane walked into the shop, and Hope caught her glancing toward James Grant, who had stood the moment Jane entered the room.

"Hi Jane," his voice was gruff as he greeted her.

"Hello, James." Jane's cheeks pinked, and Hope's brow furrowed as she caught a definite vibe between them. "Here's the order you came for."

She put the box on the counter and slid it to him with the list folded and taped to the top.

"Thank you." James pulled some notes out of his pocket.

"Wait, I need the note to ring up the sale," Hope said.

"Here you go," Jane handed Hope a copy of the list. "I made a copy of it and ticked all the items in the box." She smiled at Hope. "Of course, you're welcome to check the box."

"No!" Hope felt awful that Jane thought she didn't trust her. "I'm sure you've filled the order."

Jane gave Hope another smile which faded as she turned. Her voice grew frosty when she addressed James this time, "Please let Mrs. Williams know I *won't* be doing any more baking favors for her like the one she foisted on me yesterday."

"Okay," James' brow creased briefly before he nodded. "I didn't realize she'd done that." His voice was low. "I'm sorry. She shouldn't have inconvenienced you like that."

Hope's frown deepened at the exchange, and she felt they

were no longer discussing food. Jane gave him a nod and flounced into the kitchen while Hope rang up the sale.

"Thank you for your business," Hope gave James the receipt.

"Thank you." James nodded, picked up the box, and left.

Hope watched him go as another customer walked in.

"Oh, dear," the woman said, bending down and scooping up some paper from the floor, which she brought to Hope. "That gentleman dropped his receipt."

She handed it to Hope, who took it from the lady. Her eyes widened when she realized it was the list Jane had taped to the pastry box.

"Thank you," Hope said to the woman as she slid the folded list into her pocket.

Hope got a strange feeling that James had deliberately dropped the note for her. She gave herself a mental shake at the thought, admonishing herself for getting too pulled into this weird mystery. Hope forced her best smile and put James Grant and the Williams family from her mind to see to her customers. She made a mental note to ask her mother about her fight with Mrs. Williams all those years ago. Maybe if it was Mrs. Williams threatening Hope, it had something to do with that.

Not long after James left, Brenda relieved Hope, who entered her office and closed the door. She pulled the list James had dropped from her pocket and unfolded it. Her blood went cold as she noticed it wasn't the list but a note from Jane to Mrs. Williams.

I'm done being your spy and delivery person. Do what you want. I no longer care, and I'm going to tell the truth!

Hope pulled out her phone, took a picture of the note,

and sent it to Lance with a message that she urgently needed to see him at the bakery. She turned to look through her office window into the bakery, where Jane was busy icing some cupcakes. That feeling of unease that had settled on her that morning returned. There were not only bugs in her building but a spy as well, and another thought dawned on her.

What about Brenda? Is she friends with Gloria Williams as well? Hope knew her parents, Brenda and Gloria, all grew up and went to school together in Bar Harbor. Her eyes widened as suspicion started to grow inside Hope. Was Brenda asking for her job back to spy on Hope?

"Stop it, Hope!" She hissed under her breath. "Good grief, you're becoming far too paranoid." She closed her eyes and pinched the bridge of her nose. "Why is Gloria Williams having me spied on?"

Her office door flew open. Hope yelped as her heart thudded and a spurt of adrenaline pumped through her veins, making them race.

"Hope!" Lance looked at her, startled by her reaction. "Are you okay?"

He stepped into the office, closing the door behind him.

"Have you heard of knocking?" Hope hissed.

"I did knock," Lance told her. "I peeked through the window and saw you pinching your nose. I thought you were in pain."

"Oh!" Hope's eyes widened, and her brows shot up. "I'm sorry I didn't hear you."

"Clearly!" Lance sat down in front of her. "I got your message and got here as soon as I could."

Hope looked at the clock over her door, "Where were you?" She frowned, noting it hadn't even been eight minutes since she sent the message to Lance. "Camped out in my driveway?"

"No," Lance shook his head. "I was investigating why the silent alarm in Marli's shop was going off."

"Did her shop assistant, Debbie, trip it again?" Hope shook her head in exasperation. "Marli has told her not to put her purse near it."

"No, it wasn't Debbie," Lance told her. "She's off for the afternoon and closed up the shop."

"She did what?" Hope spluttered. "Marli is going to be furious."

"Debbie's sister had to be rushed to the hospital," Lance explained. "There was an accident of sorts."

"Oh, no," Hope said, feeling awful about what she'd just said.

"Her sister is going to be fine," Lance assured Hope. "But something or someone tripped the alarm, so I went to investigate, but it must've been her cat."

"Marli doesn't have a cat," Hope said, her brow crinkling into a frown. "We share my cat, Morris."

"Then whose cat is that monstrous black and white striped cat with the extra long legs that leaped at me the moment I stepped into the shop?" Lance asked her.

"Oh, no," Hope sighed. "That's Stiltz. Did she have one green eye and one yellow eye?"

"I'm not sure," Lance said. "I was too busy jumping out of the way of the flying ninja cat with bared claws and fangs."

Hope pursed her lips, trying not to laugh at the image Lance had just portrayed or imagining his shock when it happened.

"Are you laughing?" Lance looked at her, mortified. "Stiltz is a rather large cat for a domestic cat. In fact, I thought she was a baby mountain lion."

"In Bar Harbor?" Hope couldn't help the small snort that escaped her lips. "I'm sorry!" She cleared her throat and held up her hands. "Stiltz is rather large. But she's not that domesticated as she is a wild cat or rather a stray that the shops in the street feed."

"If she's stray, why not get animal control to collect her?" Lance asked.

"Because she's good at pest control...." Hope pursed her lips again as she stifled a giggle. "And potential burglars, it seems."

"Funny." Lance's eyes narrowed. "Stiltz drama aside, there was no one in the shop, so it must've been the cat that set it off."

"If Stiltz was in Marli's shop, then Debbie must've left a window open," Hope said. "I'll go around later and ensure it's all closed up."

"I'll go with you," Lance offered. "When we're done here."

"What do you make of the message I sent you?" Hope said softly, leaning forward on her desk.

"I'm not sure she has the skills to plant the bugs I found in your building," Lance told her. "But she certainly has the means to and could have let the bodyguard into your building."

"I think Mrs. Williams is holding something over Jane to make her do this," Hope stuck up for her employee. "I wonder what truth Jane was talking about and who she's going to tell?"

"Can I have the original note?" Lance asked Hope, who nodded and slid it over to him.

Lance had just sat back and opened the folded note when the door to Hope's office flew open, and Jane stood at the door.

"Hope can I talk to...." Jane's eyes widened as she saw the note in Lance's hand. "I see Lance beat me to it."

Jane looked around the kitchen before stepping into the office and closing the door. She turned and looked around the office as if trying to find something.

"Are you looking for the bugs that James planted?" Hope asked her.

"James?" Jane's brow furrowed. "No, he'd never do that."

"Why don't you take a seat, Jane," Lance pulled the one next to him out for her to sit down. "You can rest easy because I've already got the bugs out of the office."

"Jane!" Hope spluttered. "Why would you do this?"

"Hope!" Lance gave her a warning look. "Would you mind if I asked the questions?"

She glared at him for a few seconds before sitting back and folding her arms.

"I can explain why I let Mrs. Williams's contractor in to plant the bugs and—" Jane began, only to be interrupted by Lance.

"Contractor?" Lance looked at her questioningly. "Do you know who it was and when?"

Jane nodded. "Two weeks ago." She squinted thoughtfully. "I don't know the man's name, but I think he works for the Halls."

"What?" Lance and Hope exclaimed simultaneously.

"Do you mean Winston?" Hope looked at Jane in disbelief. "The Hall's estate manager, butler, and chauffeur?"

"I think you should add a contractor to that list," Lance glanced at Hope, pulling out his phone and flipping through some pictures. "Is that the contractor?"

"Yes, that's him," Jane nodded, pointing at the photo of Winston opening a car door for Lavinia Hall.

CHAPTER TWELVE

Logan was messaging a cab to fetch him from the hospital as he walked toward the front entrance of the hospital. He'd been relieved that Randal Manning, the lab technician he went to school with now ran the lab at Bar Harbor General Hospital. Another twinge of guilt surged through Logan over what he'd just done. But he ruthlessly pushed it aside, reminding himself that it was the only way he'd get a definite answer.

Logan knew he could rely on Randal's discretion to do the paternity test for him. He was just about to hit send on his request for a cab when he was stopped dead in his tracks near the front door of the hospital. His heart lurched into his throat as his pulse picked up speed when he saw Clair Wright struggling to carry a young girl into the front lobby.

"Come on, sweetheart." Clair Wright rushed into the hospital, struggling to carry the little girl in her arms, draped around her shoulders. "We're almost here."

"Mrs. Wright?" Logan's voice had her snapping her head around. "Can I help you?" He walked toward her.

"Logan!" Clair's eyes widened in shock, and her face paled. "I...."

“Gran-gran, I don’t feel good,” Sydney raised her head, turned it to one side, and vomited.

“Oh, no!” Clair’s voice raised slightly, vibrating with panic. Her eyes scanned the entrance hall. “I need a doctor.”

“Please, let me help you.” Logan quelled the churning in his stomach and the thudding of his heart when he’d seen how pale Sydney was.

Clair nodded as he approached them. “If you could just hold her while I get a doctor.” She said, “I fear my legs and arms will break.”

Logan nodded and hooked his cane over his arm as he held them out for Clair to pass Sydney to him.

“Gran?” Sydney looked at her in alarm.

“It’s okay, sweetheart. This is Logan.” She smiled warmly at the child before handing her to him. “He’s Nanna Lavinia’s grandson.”

“Oh,” Sydney nodded before turning to look at Logan shyly. “Hello.” Her voice was weak, and his heart lurched when she grabbed her stomach in pain. “Ow, Gran-gran, it hurts.” She looked at Clair.

Logan had been floored by the child's big blue eyes and her pretty face that was splattered by freckles that stood out more because of how ashen Sydney was.

“I know, my love, I know,” Clair’s voice was filled with emotion. “I need you to go to Logan so Gran-gran can find us a doctor. Is that okay?”

Sydney nodded, and Clair passed her to Logan. He felt as if his heart would burst when the child turned and wrapped her arms around his neck. Logan was alarmed at how hot she was.

“She’s burning up,” Logan said to Clair, who nodded.

“Are you going to be okay holding her?” Clair looked pointedly at his leg.

“I’ll be fine,” Logan insisted, his arms winding possessively around Sydney as she put her head on his shoulder. "Let's go find a doctor."

Logan ignored the searing pain in his side and forced himself to limp alongside Clair as they went to the front desk.

"We need a doctor urgently," Clair told the woman manning the desk. "My granddaughter is ill. She's been vomiting, and her stomach is in excruciating pain."

"I'm going to need you to fill this out," the woman handed her a clipboard with a form attached. "While you start on that, I'll page a doctor." The woman said as Logan was about to voice his annoyance in filling out a form before Sydney saw a doctor.

"Oh, and she got sick near the front door," Clair pointed over her shoulder as she picked up the clipboard.

"I'll get someone to clean that up as well," the woman told them.

Within a couple of minutes, two nurses wheeling a gurney walked toward them.

"Is this the patient with acute abdominal pain?" the one nurse asked and looked at Logan, who nodded.

"Are you her father?" the nurse asked Logan, who froze and didn't know how to answer.

"He's a close family friend," Clair told her. "I'm the grandmother, and Logan is with us."

"Fine," the nurse said. "Sir, can you please put her on the bed?"

Logan was reluctant to let her go.

"No, I want to stay with Logan," Sydney didn't want to let him go either, it seemed, and Logan felt his heart expand.

"Sweetie, we have to put you on the bed and take you to the examination room," the nurse explained to Sydney. "Your grandmother and...." She looked at him inquiringly.

"Logan," he filled in for her.

"Logan will be right there, I promise," the nurse gently rubbed Sydney's back. "I'm sure you want to feel better?"

Sydney nodded before pushing herself up and reaching over to the nurse. When Logan let her go, he had the most profound feeling of loss and gave himself a mental shake. The nurse lay her gently on the bed, kicked off the brake, and they started wheeling Sydney down the passage into a room.

Logan and Clair stood in the room near the window and waved at Sydney when the nurse pointed to where they were.

"She doesn't like being alone," Clair's voice was hoarse with emotion, and Logan saw tears in her eyes. "This is all my fault." She pulled a tissue from her pocket. "Hope told me to keep Sydney at home and not let her have too much excitement." She dabbed her eyes. "So what do I do? I took Sydney shopping."

"It's not your fault, Clair," Logan assured her. "I've been told children get sick all the time."

"But, Logan, she's really, really sick," Clair looked at her granddaughter as the nurses worked.

"Mrs. Wright?" A tall elderly man with a tablet in his hand walked into the room and approached them.

"That's me," Clair stepped around Logan.

"I'm Doctor Trask, and I'll be caring for Sydney," the doctor introduced himself. "I've got her records from her pediatrician, and I see she has a rare blood type?"

"Yes, she has," Clair confirmed. "There is a donor on the island that donates blood regularly." Her eyes slid nervously to Logan before looking at Doctor Trask again. "So there should be blood if she needs it."

"I see that." Doctor Trask nodded and looked at Logan. "Are you the father?"

"He's a family friend," Clair introduced them.

"Logan Hall," he introduced himself to the doctor. "May I ask what blood type?" He looked at Clair, who nodded her permission.

"She's RH Null," Doctor Trask told him. "Did you say,

Logan Hall?" He flipped through his charts. "You're the other RH Null blood donor's grandson?"

"If you're talking about Rod Hall, then yes, he is my grandfather, and I'm the same blood type as him," Logan told the doctor.

"Great," Doctor Trask nodded. "I'll tell you how Sydney is in a few minutes."

The doctor turned and walked to Sydney's bed while an awkward silence fell between Clair and Logan.

"Does Hope know you've brought Sydney to the hospital?" Logan asked Clair, wanting to break up the awkwardness.

"I did, but her phone just goes straight to voicemail," Clair said. "I hated to break the news to her with a message, but I had no option. She wasn't answering her phone."

"I'll try to call her," Logan offered, pulling out his phone.

"No!" Clair said a little too quickly, grabbing his hand to stop him. "You stay with Sydney, I'll do it." She looked at Sydney.

"I'll be right here," Logan promised.

"Thank you." Clair gave him a tight smile before pulling her phone from her purse and walking out the room.

She was about to walk away when a commotion from the hallway caught their attention and Logan popped his head out the room.

"Mom?" Hope's voice rang out to them as they turned to see her, with Lance in tow, heading for them.

Logan knew it was irrational, but a surge of hot jealousy at seeing Hope and Lance together surged through him. He had a feeling Hope barely noticed him until she was right on top of him.

"Logan?" Hope looked at him standing in the ward doorway in surprise. "What are you doing here?"

"He helped me with Sydney because I couldn't carry her,"

Clair explained and was saved from having to say more when Doctor Trask walked up to them.

"Doctor Trask?" Hope looked at him, confused. "Where is Doctor Meldan, Sydney's regular doctor?"

"Doctor Meldan is off sick," Doctor Trask explained. "Even if he wasn't, he would've called me because Sydney has acute appendicitis, and we need to operate."

"What?" Clair, Hope, and Logan all said at once.

"I will need parental consent," Doctor Trask looked at Hope, who nodded. "Good. The nurse will bring you the forms to fill out. You can go sit with her while we prepare for surgery."

"You're doing it now?" Hope asked, her face going ashen.

"I'm afraid we have to. We can't risk it bursting," Doctor Trask told her. "Now, if you'll excuse me, I must prepare for the surgery. The nurses will answer any questions you may have."

The doctor turned and walked off, leaving them standing, staring dumbly after him.

"Oh, Hope, I'm so sorry, my darling!" Clair wailed.

"It's not your fault, Mom. This would've happened if she was with you or me," Hope pointed out. "If you'll excuse me. I'd like to spend some time with my daughter."

Lance, Clair, and Logan nodded, then stepped aside for Hope to enter the room. It was hard for Logan not to demand that he be allowed to stay in the room too. But he refrained from doing so and contented himself watching mother and child through the window.

"Clair?" Lavinia's voice had them all turning to look down the hall once again.

"Grandmother?" Logan squinted as he saw his grandparents rushing toward them.

"Logan?" Lavinia eyed him warily. "What are you doing here?"

"Logan found me struggling to get Sydney into the

hospital and helped me carry her," Clair explained. "Thank you for coming." She reached out and squeezed Lavinia's hand.

"Of course, we'd be here, just in case she needed...." Lavinia glanced uncomfortably at Logan. "Support. She needed support."

Logan's eyes narrowed, and he shook his head, not believing that his grandparents knew who Sydney was to him and had not said a word about her. Anger washed over him at being lied to by the two people he trusted the most. Logan balled his fists at his side and clenched his jaw as he held onto it breathing slowly to calm himself down.

His eyes slid to the little girl lying in the big hospital bed, being comforted by her mother. His anger instantly subsided at the sight. Tears burned the back of his eyes when he thought of Sydney in pain. He knew that he'd change places with her in a heartbeat if he could. Even by some odd chance, if she wasn't his daughter, she was part of Hope, and Logan knew as soon as he'd seen Hope running toward them that he loved her more than ever.

Logan swallowed the lump in his throat and leaned heavily on his cane, overwhelmed by his feelings for the two ladies in the room before him. The conversation he'd had with Melissa earlier that day flashed through his mind as her words resonated through him.

And don't pretend you didn't know how your mother helped you get out of that mess with Chase's little sister all those years ago!

His brow knotted as flashes of his farewell party seven years ago ran before his eyes. Logan had been nervous and trying to avoid Hope because he didn't want to ruin the surprise he had for her the following day. As soon as he knew what he needed for that day was ready, Logan had wanted to pull her into his arms and —

"Logan!" Lavinia's voice was slightly raised. "Honey, where

did you go?" She looked at him worriedly. "I've asked you if you wanted a coffee three times."

"Sorry," Logan said, shaking his head. "I've got a lot on my mind."

Logan's eyes slid to Lance. He hadn't said much since he'd arrived with Hope. Instead, he'd been furiously working on his phone.

What is Lance doing with Hope? Logan wondered. *Are they dating?* He nearly spluttered when the thought hit him.

Logan's eyes narrowed as he watched the man, and he was sure he'd heard that Lance was engaged to a Maine socialite.

Is that engagement over? Now Lance is in a relationship with Hope?

"You still haven't answered me, sweetheart," Lavinia reminded him. "I'm about to go on a coffee run."

"I'd like a bottle of water. Thanks, Grandmother," Logan answered, turning his tormented thoughts away from Lance and Hope's relationship status.

"What about something to eat?" Lavinia asked him. "We may be here for a while."

"Oh, please, you don't all have to stay," Clair told them.

"We want to," Logan answered for the Hall family and looked at Lance questioningly.

"I have to leave," Lance told them, looking into the room. "Would you please tell Hope to let me know how little Syd is?"

"Of course, I will," Clair assured Lance.

He said his goodbyes, and Logan felt relief flood him when the man left. He liked Lance. They had been good friends when they were young, even though they ran in a different crowd. Lance was friends with the Rivers family, Chase and Hope's cousins. So Lance was always around at the functions and events that involved all their families. Logan also knew Lance was helping Bradley with the case of figuring out who was threatening Hope and silently stalking him.

When the medical staff came to take Sydney for her operation, Lavinia had just returned with the coffee order. Clair, Lavinia, and Rod kissed her cheek, squeezed her, and promised to be here when she woke up as they wheeled Sydney's bed out of the room. His heart skipped a few beats when Sydney reached out and took Logan's hand.

"Will you walk with Mommy and me?" Sydney asked him, groggy from the pre-med pill they had given her.

Logan's head shot up, and his eyes connected with Hope's. She was staring at him in surprise at her daughter's actions.

"If it's okay with your mom?" Logan dragged his eyes away from Hope's to smile at Sydney.

"Is it okay, Mommy?" Sydney turned to look at her mom, whose hand she was also holding.

"Uh..." Hope cleared her throat. "Sure, baby."

They walked with Sydney as far as the medical staff would let them go. Hope kissed and squeezed Sydney, promising to be there when she opened her eyes. Sydney surprised them both by asking Logan if he'd be there too, and he promised her he would.

Logan and Hope stood side by side, watching Sydney being wheeled away until their view of her was cut off when the large green doors slammed shut. He wasn't sure what he was supposed to do after that. All he knew at that moment was that he had a huge knot in his stomach, and worry was pounding through his veins.

"Thank you." Hope's soft voice caught his attention, and their eyes locked. "For helping my mother with Sydney and being so good with her." She gave him a tight smile, and his heart went out to her when he saw her fighting back the tears.

"It's going to be okay," Logan assured her, instinctively reaching out and taking her hands. "She's tough, like her mother." He smiled.

Hope pursed her lips and nodded but couldn't stop a stray tear from spilling over her bottom lid.

"Hey!" Logan's voice softened, and he reached up to wipe the tear away. "We're going to be right here when she comes out."

Hope nodded again, and before he knew what he was doing, he pulled her to him, wrapping his arms around her, feeling her body shake slightly as she sniffed. Logan didn't know how long they stood there like that and didn't care who saw them. It felt so good to hold her again. To draw comfort from her and give comfort back as they waited anxiously for Sydney's operation to be over.

"Logan?" Chase's voice boomed down the hospital's quiet sterile halls, making him and Hope spring apart to stare guiltily at his best friend and Hope's brother.

"Chase!" Hope breathed and ran into her brother's arms. "Oh, it's so good to see you. I'm sorry we couldn't be at the ferry to greet you."

"I understand," Chase's eyes narrowed as he looked over Hope's shoulder to Logan. "Thorn picked me up. He's here with the kids in the waiting room."

"Oh!" Hope's head turned toward the direction of the waiting room.

"How is she?" Chase asked Hope.

"I don't know," Hope sniffed and swiped at her cheek.

"She's going to be okay," Chase promised. "Just like she was when she had her tonsils out."

Hope nodded. "I best go say hello to Thorn and the kids."

"Okay." Chase kissed her forehead.

As Hope rounded the corner out of view, Chase turned on him before Logan could say anything.

"What the heck was that with my sister?" Chase hissed. "Is there something I should know about?"

"Something *you* should know about?" Logan looked at his

lifelong best friend in disbelief. "Shouldn't I be the one asking *you* that?"

"What is that supposed to mean?" Chase frowned, confused before something dawned on him. "Did Rose tell you about Hazel?"

"What?" Logan's face scrunched up. It was his turn to be confused. "What has Hazel got to do with this?"

Chase drew back his head and chin as he eyed Logan warily. "Hazel and I were going to get engaged before she left me two years ago."

"You told me, remember?" Logan reminded him. "The night you broke your nose, and I had to take you to the hospital, you were doped up with pain pills."

"Then I don't understand what you mean by what I should be telling you?" Chase's eyes narrowed angrily once again. "I wasn't the one caught in an intimate position with your sister."

"I'm talking about me being Sydney's father!" Logan hissed. "It's bad enough that my grandparents have kept this a secret from me for all these years." His eyes burned with anger. "But I didn't expect it from you!"

Logan's eyes widened as he watched Chase's expression turn from anger to shocked surprise. Chase stood staring in disbelief as Logan's words sank in.

"You're Sydney's father?" Chase rasped.

"You didn't know?" Logan said with a frown and shook his head in disbelief.

"No, he did not!" Thorn's voice, although low, snapped like a whip through the air. "This is not the time or place for the two of you to air your grievances."

Before anyone could say anything else, a nurse burst through the doors, stopped in front of the three of them, and asked, "Which one of you is Logan Hall?"

"Him!" Thorn and Chase said simultaneously.

They pointed to Logan, who held up his hand and said, "That's me."

"I believe you are the same blood type as Sydney Wright?" the nurse asked Logan and he nodded. "Do you know of any reason why you couldn't give blood?"

"No," Logan shook his head. His heart had started hammering loudly in his chest.

"Are you able to give a few pints of blood?" the nurse asked him. "We may need it."

Logan looked from Chase to Thorn, staring at him wide-eyed, before he looked at the nurse.

"Yes," Logan said before following the nurse through the green doors Sydney had disappeared through.

CHAPTER THIRTEEN

Hope paced back and forth in the small waiting room. Her mother and Lavinia were sitting beside each other on the chairs that lined the wall. Rod was in the children's play section building houses with blocks with Thorn's children, Aaron and Tate. Hope's mind was in turmoil, and her stomach was in knots. She felt physically ill with worry for Sydney. She was also anxious for her brothers to return because she didn't know what was happening between them and Logan.

This is a fine mess you've made of things, Hope! she admonished herself. *Everyone who knows about Sydney warned you this was going to happen.*

Hope stopped at the one end of the room, closed her eyes, blew out a breath, and rubbed her palm against her forehead. She needed to find out what was happening with her brothers and Logan. Hope was anxious enough about Sydney. She couldn't worry about Logan and her brothers as well. Chase did not look happy catching Hope in Logan's arms. She knew he'd never understand and that he'd react that way. Hope's older brothers had always been overly protective of her. The three of them had a silent sibling understanding — *No dating each other's friends*. Especially not best friends.

Hope didn't have a problem with any of her brothers being interested in her best friend because her best friend was their cousin Marli. But she had broken their silent understanding years before when Hope and Logan had a secret summer relationship. Hope had a crush on Logan since she'd started noticing boys. She'd dated before her brief relationship with Logan and again after when Sydney was two. But Hope didn't feel it was fair for her to date until her daughter was old enough. Marli had told Hope she thought it was a cop-out because Hope was afraid to get her heart broken again.

Marli was partly right. Hope never wanted to have to go through the kind of heartache she'd done with Logan ever again. Hope had channeled all her love into her daughter and had no room for anyone else. That was until Logan breezed back into town and turned her life upside down. Now she was being spied on, threatened, and found herself thinking about him all day and night. The few times they'd run into each other her heart had nearly pounded out of her chest as it reached out for his. While Hope was trying to get her wayward emotions under control, she couldn't help but admit how good it had felt to be held by him again.

She was snapped out of her thoughts by Thorn and Chase entering the room.

"Hope!" Thorn made a beeline for her. She could see by the look on his face something was wrong. He'd had that same look the night he'd told them about their father.

"What's happened?" Hope breathed, her eyes widening in despair.

She looked past her brothers and noted Logan wasn't with them.

"Where's Logan?" Hope asked Thorn. "What did the two

of you do?" Her eyes narrowed accusingly. "He was just being nice to me."

"Hope!" Thorn reached out and grabbed the top of her arms, stilling her. "Logan is fine." He shook his head. "Or at least I think he is."

"You think he is?" Hope frowned.

"A nurse took him into a room near the theaters," Thorn told her.

"What?" Fear bolted through Hope. "Why?"

"They needed him to give some blood," Thorn told her calmly. "Now, before you panic." His grip on her arms tightened. "I managed to find a nurse who went and checked for us." His eyebrows raised. "It was just a precautionary measure because a few pints of Rod's blood got tainted when one of the storage fridges broke down a few days ago."

"But how did Logan know....." Hope's voice trailed off, and her head shot around to see Lavinia and her mother watching her intently. "You told him?"

"No, not me!" Lavinia held up her hands defensively. "And I know Rod didn't either. We've hardly seen him since we've been back; he's been out the whole day."

"I think he figured it out," Clair explained. "Doctor Trask asked me about Sydney's blood type and Logan asked what it was. And the doctor made the connection between Logan and Rod."

"So he doesn't know." Hope looked at the two women hopefully.

"Hone.," Lavinia and Clair exchanged a look. "He's not stupid, sweetheart."

"There are only two other people in Bar Harbor with that blood type, and he knows he inherited it from his grandfather," Clair said. "And honey, Syd looks more and more like her father every day."

"So it's true!" Chase, who had been silently listening, glared at Hope. "All these years, I've been harboring this anger towards the idiot that left you alone and pregnant—" His eyes darkened angrily. "And it turns out he's been right in front of me the entire time."

"I'm sorry, Chase." Hope stepped around Thorn and walked toward him. "This is the reason why I didn't tell you."

She reached out to take his hand, but he pulled away. Hurt and anger boiled in his eyes.

"Don't!" Chase hissed and looked around the room. "You all lied to me this whole time."

"Chase, sweetie." Clair stood up and walked to him, but he pulled away from her too.

"No!" He pointed rudely at her. "You're my mother!" He shook his head and then looked at Thorn. "Can I have your car keys?"

"I'll take you home," Thorn offered. "You shouldn't be driving when you're this angry."

"I'm not driving," Chase told them. "Turns out, my only friend, Rose, didn't know about Hope and Logan either." He glared at them. "She's coming to get me."

"I'll get your bags," Thorn told him. "Why don't you stay here and work this out?"

"I need time to think this through," Chase told them and looked at Hope, his eyes softening. "Please let me know how Syd is doing."

Hope stood staring at her brother and nodded. A lump formed in her throat as she fought back the tears. The pain in her heart grew, as did the sickening knot in her stomach. Chase stared at her cooly for a few more seconds. Then he spun on his heel and stormed out of the room. Thorn started to follow him but stopped beside Hope.

"Don't worry, he'll cool down," Thorn assured her.

"I don't know about that," Hope said. "I've never seen Chase look so hurt and angry before."

"He's going through a lot right now," Thorn, always the

one to try to keep everyone together, told her. "Just give him time."

Hope nodded as her brother leaned in and kissed her forehead. "Keep an eye on my kids for me?" he asked her softly. "I don't want them tiring Rod."

"Sure," Hope promised, watching her oldest brother exit the room.

"Are you alright, honey?" Lavinia asked.

"What have I done?" Hope put her hands on her hips and dropped her head back, staring up at the ceiling. "What was I thinking trying to keep this a secret?" She threw her hands in the air and looked at the two women staring at her. "I know what you're thinking!"

"Hope, we're not thinking anything," Clair assured her.

But Hope ignored her mother, lost in her own agony and torment. "You all warned me to get ahead of my secret before it got out!" She threw her arms in the air and started to pace as she mumbled. "It's not that I didn't want to tell Logan or Chase." She stopped and looked at Clair and Lavinia. "I have an entire notepad with letters I started writing to both of them."

"We believe you, honey," Lavinia's voice was soft and soothing. "Now, please, will you sit down?" She patted the seat next to her. "You're going to make yourself ill."

"I've hurt Logan, I've hurt Chase...." Hope's voice trailed off as it caught in her throat. Tears sprang to her eyes as she felt a crushing weight pressing down on her chest. "Oh, my word—" She looked at her mother and Lavinia. "Worst of all, I've hurt my baby."

The tears started to drip down her cheeks as the weight on her chest got heavier, and her breathing got harder. Hope leaned forward with her hands on her knees, trying to catch her breath. She started to feel giddy as the world throbbed around her.

"Hope!" Clair sprang to her feet alongside Lavinia to rush to Hope's side.

"You're having a panic attack," Lavinia explained, looking around the room. "Is there a paper bag around here?"

"I'll get one," Rod offered. "The kids are asleep in the playroom." He told them before leaving.

"Come sit down." Clair helped Lavinia guide Hope to a chair. "You have to breathe, honey."

"I...." Hope panted. "I can't!" She looked at her mother wide-eyed. "I can't."

"Yes, you can," Lavinia kneeled in front of her, putting her hands on Hope's thighs. "Look at me." She held Hope's gaze. "Now, breathe in through your nose." She demonstrated. "And out through your mouth."

Hope followed Lavinia's lead, and soon her airway opened up and she could breathe again.

"I can't find a paper bag or nurse anywhere!" Rod said frustratedly as he walked into the room. "Is everything alright now?"

"Yes, thank you, Rod," Clair smiled at him. "I think we have the attack under control."

Hope saw Rod standing watching her for a few seconds. When Lavinia stood up and sat beside her, he took the seat in front of her.

"Hope, I understand why you did what you did," Rod smiled warmly at her. "Heck, if I was in your shoes, I'd probably have done the same thing."

"He did do something similar," Lavinia told Hope. "Well, not having a baby part." She made them laugh. "But when Rod and I first fell in love, I was engaged to another man."

"She was," Rod confirmed. "Not just any man but my older brother."

"You were engaged to Dean Hall?" Clair spluttered. "From the rock band Hall of Fame? That Dean Hall?"

"I was," Lavinia smiled at Clair. "But I knew I was with the wrong man the moment I met Rod."

"I won't get into the long story," Rod told her. "But Dean had been having an affair behind Lavinia's back and fathered a child with the woman."

"Rod, being loyal to his brother, kept his secret," Lavinia continued. "But as with all secrets, Dean's was revealed when the woman was no longer content to be the other woman."

"Only when this secret came out, it wasn't Dean's career that got hurt. It was Lavinia's," Rod told them. "That woman went public with her relationship with Dean and slandered Lavinia."

"She made me out to be a monster." Lavinia's eyes misted over. "It was the worst time of my life, and to make it a lot worse."She looked at her husband. "Rod had to protect his record label and back his brother."

"But I started a new label that included a movie studio, and I put all my time and effort into rebuilding Lavinia's career," Rod told them. "It took another year or two before she trusted me again, but I won her over in the end." He looked at Hope. "As soon as she fell pregnant, like you, we didn't want our child raised in the spotlight. So Lavinia hung up her guitar, and I semi-retired the producing business to live in Bar Harbor."

"We too, went overboard, trying to protect Stan from the press and the heavy burden of living in the stardom fishbowl," Lavinia told her. "But look how that turned out for us."

"Our son became a famous movie star, took over the studio business, and married a superstar." Rod gave a laugh and shook his head. "We were so glad when Logan didn't want that life. But he will always get sucked into it because of his parents."

"And, Hope," Clair got into the conversation. "The moment you got involved with Logan, You were spinning on the rim of the tidal pool of that world."

"So what you're saying is everything I've done to protect my daughter was in vain?" Hope leaned her head against the wall.

"No, not at all," Lavinia stressed. "Rod and I admire everything you've done to keep Sydney having a normal life."

"But she's getting older," Rod told her. "We didn't want to say anything, but she's asked us a few times in these past few months about our relationship with her and if we're her real grandparents like Clair is."

"She has?" Hope sat up and looked at them in shock.

"Yes, baby girl," Clair confirmed. "She's asked me as well."

"And none of you said anything?" Hope looked at them in disbelief.

"You've had so much to deal with, with your business expansion and the apartment renovations," Clair told her. "We thought it best not to worry you, and we handled it."

"How did you handle it?" Hope stared at the three of them wide-eyed.

"The three of us discussed it. We decided to be as honest as we could with Sydney without violating your trust or overstepping our boundaries," Lavinia told her.

"Lavinia and I told her we were her real great-grandparents," Rod said honestly.

"She never questioned how we were related," Lavinia explained.

"I said the same thing," Clair assured her.

"Oh, this is just great!" That weight was pressing down on her chest again. "What have I done?" She stared at the roof. "I should've just been upfront with her about her father."

"Why?" Thorn's voice startled her.

She'd been so engrossed in her misery and failure as a mother that she hadn't heard him come back into the room.

"Sydney is a well-adjusted and happy little girl," Thorn walked over to them and sat next to Rod. "According to Aaron, who has asked her a few times about her father, she looks to you as her complete parental unit." He took his sister's hand. "I believe she told Aaron that one day when Sydney was ready to or felt she needed to, she'd ask you about him."

"Sydney said that to Aaron?" Hope asked, amazed. "She's only six."

"And look how well-balanced and loved she feels," Thorn pointed out.

"Thank you." Hope gave her brother a grateful smile. "All of you." She took her mother's and Lavinia's hands and looked at Rod. "The four of you have been my rocks through these years. You've supported me, had my back, and were always there for Syd and me."

"Oh, honey, we wouldn't have had it any other way," Lavinia, Rod, Thorn, and Clair assured her.

"If you want my advice," Thorn said to her. "Tonight, and until you're happy she's out of the woods, Sydney is your only priority."

"I agree with Thorn," Lavinia said, with Clair and Rod backing her up.

"But Logan has figured it out, and I think, if he wants to, you need to let him be a part of Sydney's recovery," Thorn suggested. "After that, you can play it by ear as to when the two of you sit down and have a good talk."

"Your brother is giving you excellent advice," Rod told her. "I know my grandson, and now that he knows, he will want to be there for Sydney.

Hope nodded and pursed her lips, "Okay." She blew out a breath and then looked at Thorn. "But what about Chase?" She cleared her throat. "I've blown up his friendship with Logan and caused this big rift between the family."

"Give him time." Clair patted her daughter's leg. "He'll come around. You know what he's like." She smiled reassuringly. "Chase and Logan have been through so much that they will find their way back together as friends again."

"I agree with Mom," Thorn told Hope. "Let Chase simmer down, and he'll come back."

Before they could say more, the doctor walked into the room followed by Logan.

"Sydney's in the recovery room," Doctor Trask told them. "The operation was a success. We managed to get the appendix out before it burst."

"Thank you, doctor." Hope got up.

"The nurse will come to get you when you can see her." Doctor Trask left them.

"Logan, are you okay?" Lavinia went over to her grandson.

"I'm fine," Logan hobbled over to them, his eyes locked with Hope's. "I'm just glad that Sydney is going to be okay."

"Thank you for giving blood," Hope said, feeling awkward.

"I didn't end up giving blood," Logan told them. "They did take a bit. But just to test it. Then I had to wait in case they needed me." He gave Hope a smile. "I've agreed to return in the morning and donate blood."

"I'll come with him," Rod told Logan. "The hospital did call me today to let me know what happened to their storage fridge."

"Thank you." Hope looked at them both as a nurse came to call her.

"Miss Wright," the nurse looked at Hope. "You can see your daughter now."

Hope stood up and looked at Logan. "Would you like to come with me?"

Logan looked startled for a few seconds before nodding and following Hope from the room, taking the olive branch she'd extended him.

CHAPTER FOURTEEN

Logan and Hope walked into Sydney's room together as she pushed open her heavy lids.

"Mommy?" Sydney's voice was rough with sleep.

"Hello, sweetheart," Hope's voice wobbled with emotion. Her eyes were glassy with unshed tears as she leaned over and kissed Sydney's forehead.

Logan walked into the room but kept a little distance between himself and the bed so the nurse could work around him. He felt the tightly wound knot in his belly loosen when Sydney smiled at Hope.

"I'm thirsty." Sydney swallowed. "My throat is raspy."

"She can have small sips of water," the nurse instructed, handing Hope a bottle of water with a straw in it. "Make sure she doesn't drink too fast or too much, or she may get sick."

"Thank you," Hope smiled at the elderly nurse.

Hope propped Sydney up with one arm and put the straw to her daughter's lips.

"You heard the nurse, baby," Hope's voice was soft and soothing. "Just small sips, okay?"

Sydney nodded as she drank from the straw.

"Hey there, sleepy head." The nurse smiled at Sydney as

she propped the bed up, so Sydney's head was slightly raised. "You did so well in your operation, and now that nasty appendix making you sick is gone."

"Then why is my tummy still sore?" Sydney asked her, watching the nurse fuss about the room and check her vitals.

"It's going to be sore for a few days," the nurse warned her. "But that's just because of the operation that your body has to heal from."

"Oh!" Sydney rubbed her eyes. "When can I go home?"

"Maybe tomorrow," the nurse told her. "But the doctor will pay you a visit later today and again in the morning before he decides."

"That's good news." Hope smiled at Sydney.

"Barbie will be missing me," Sydney looked worriedly at Hope.

"It's okay. Uncle Thorn, Aaron, and Tate have her, and she'll stay with them until you're home," Hope explained. "And Morris will be home on Saturday too."

"Really?" Sydney's eyes widened in delight. "I've missed him so much, and I promise my marbles are all hidden."

"Who is Morris?" Logan and the nurse asked at the same time.

"He's our Siamese cat that has a thing for eating shiny things." Hope shook her head. "I think he's half magpie."

"He ate one of my marbles and had to have an operation," Sydney told them. "He's been gone for days and days."

"He got an infection, and my brother, the local vet, had to keep him longer at the animal hospital," Hope explained.

"My goodness," the nurse said to Sydney. "So you and your cat are in the hospital?"

"Yes," Sydney nodded.

"Well, if the doctor is happy with your progress tomorrow, you'll be home in time to greet Morris," the nurse assured her. "I'll be back to check on you soon, love."

"Thank you," Sydney smiled at the nurse.

"I'm down the hall at the nurse's station if you need me," the nurse's eyes moved from Hope to Sydney. "You need to rest more so your body can focus on healing."

Sydney nodded at the nurse as she left the three of them in the room.

"You stayed." Sydney's attention turned to Logan, and his heart thudded in his chest at the smile she beamed at him.

"I promised you I would." Logan cleared his throat and stepped closer to the bed.

"Thank you," Sydney said politely before covering her yawn with a little hand. "Where's gran-gran, nan, and pops?"

"We're right here, sweetie," Clair, Lavinia, and Rod piled into the room. "Uncle Thorn said I must give you a kiss from him because he had to take Aaron and Tate home and get Barbie."

Clair leaned forward and kissed Sydney on the forehead, "That one's from me, and this is from Thorn." She kissed her two more times, making Sydney giggle.

"Don't hog our girls' attention," Lavinia maneuvered between Clair and Sydney. "There's my favorite little girl."

Logan's heart caught in his throat as he saw the love in his grandparent's eyes for Sydney and the resentment he'd felt for them earlier for lying to him for six years fade. Seeing how they doted on Sydney and knowing how much Lavinia loved kids and wanted great-grandchildren, he understood why she'd done what she did. Logan knew his grandparents doted on him, too, and realized how hard it must've been for them.

To be a part of Sydney's life, they had to keep Hope's secret, although when he thought about it, they had thrown hints and clues at him over the years. Logan had been too stubborn to acknowledge them or realize they were hoping he'd guess. And as the pictures of Sydney in his grandparent's house came to mind, he realized it was kind of obvious. They had acted like proud great-grandparents and even had Sydney's music and dance trophies in a special trophy case.

Every time he'd come home for a visit in the past six years, Lavinia and Rod couldn't stop talking about Sydney. But all Logan had heard when they did was the sound of his aching heart and the cry of his bruised soul as he felt them rubbing salt in his wounds about Hope. She'd broken his heart seven years ago when she'd run off without an explanation. Logan could still feel the pain of the shock that had ripped through him when he'd seen her months later at his grandparent's house. She'd looked so radiant she'd shone with her pregnancy, making her look even more beautiful.

Logan's mind had been so clouded with anger, hurt, and her betrayal that he'd never for one moment thought Sydney had been the product of their short-lived relationship. No, that was a lie. There had been a moment when Chase had first told him that Hope was pregnant that he'd thought it. Or rather had hoped it, and his heart, mind, and soul had lurched in excitement, picturing what it would be like to have a child with Hope. But that had been a brief moment. Chase had shattered any illusion Logan may have had of him being the father when he told Logan it was Hope's boyfriend from college she'd been seeing for the past year.

Hope and Sydney's laughter caught Logan's attention as his eyes traveled to Sydney's bed. Rod was regaling them with a story. His stomach knotted watching them and feeling like a peeping Tom watching a happy family through a window wishing he was part of it. Suddenly he was finding it difficult to breathe, and the walls felt like they were closing in on him.

I have to get out of here! Beads of perspiration popped up on his brow when his phone buzzing saved him. He pulled it out of his pocket and saw it was Rose.

"Sorry, I have to take this," Logan said to no one in particular in the room and ducked out. Walking away from Sydney's room to an empty waiting room as he answered. "Hi."

"I thought you weren't going to answer. You took so long!" Rose moaned. "How did Sydney's surgery go?"

Logan told her how Sydney was and promised to send updates on her progress.

"So, you have a daughter?" Rose blurted.

"I think so," Logan's voice was filled with uncertainty.

"You *think* so?" Rose spluttered.

"I haven't been told in so many words," Logan explained.

"Well, Chase seems to think you have," Rose pointed out.

"Is he with you?" Logan already knew the answer.

"Yes, and he's pretty upset that he wasn't told about Sydney or your relationship with Hope," Rose informed him. "I'm upset that you never really told me about *everything* either."

"It's been a crazy day for me, Rose." Logan sighed. "Can we leave this for another day?"

"Sure," Rose said. "I'm sorry. I couldn't begin to imagine how this is affecting you."

"To be honest, it's still sinking in," Logan told her, closing his eyes and pinching the bridge of his nose.

"Can you tell me about it?" Rose's voice softened. "You and Hope, I mean."

"Is Chase close by?" Logan opened his eyes and stared at the blank wall before him.

"Yes, he's here," Rose told him. "I'm going to put you on speaker if that's okay?"

"Sure, why not!" Logan sighed. It was time to tell his best friends the truth. "Summer seven years ago, I fell in love with Hope and thought she felt the same way about me."

"Was Hope the one you got your great-grandmother's ring resized for that year?" Rose realized. "Hope was the girl of your dreams that was going to get your treasured heirloom?"

"Yes," Logan confirmed, rubbing his eyes. He'd forgotten he'd told Chase and Rose he'd found the one.

"We wondered what had happened as all you told us before you left for Seal training that year was that it didn't work out," Rose remembered. "The next thing Chase and I heard was that you were back together with Melissa."

"It was safe with Melissa," Logan explained. "I had been hurt by my first love and ripped apart by my second love, which just happened to be my one big and true love."

There was silence on the other end of the line for a few moments before Rose broke it and moved the conversation away from Logan's broken heart.

"I remember when you took Melissa on your first date," Rose told him.

"I only did that because Chase stole my date to the premier of Melissa, Hazel, and my mom's new movie," Logan pointed out.

"You mean the movie where Melissa stole the lead part from Hazel?" Chase's voice was laced with anger — but at least he was talking to Logan again, even if it was angrily.

"I never once disagreed with either of you about Melissa stealing Hazel's role," Logan reminded them. "I was gutted when my mother told me Hazel had asked Chase to go with her."

"What?" Chase choked. "Hazel didn't ask me. Melissa told me that Hazel didn't have a date and that you had asked Melissa to go with you."

"No!" Logan frowned. *How am I only hearing about this now? Because you didn't want to hear it when you were sixteen!* His subconscious answered back. Logan gave himself a mental shake. "Melissa told me that my mom set you and Hazel up because Hazel was too shy to ask you herself."

"That lying manipulator!" Rose hissed. "Her fans deserve to know what she's really like. This sweet, kind, caring persona she plays for the public must be stripped away once and for all."

"You never liked Melissa, Rose," Chase said to her. "Right from that first date Logan and Melissa had."

"Neither did you!" Rose pointed out and gave a short

laugh. "You were just too enamored of Hazel to say anything to Logan that first night."

"But you almost stayed away from the premier because Logan went with Melissa," Chase said.

"I would've too if your mother and mine hadn't dragged me there," Rose hissed at Chase. "Logan, you have no idea how many times Chase and I plotted to separate the two of you. We still think she is evil."

"I noticed your schemes," Logan admitted. "And Melissa isn't that bad."

"No, she's much worse!" Rose stated. "We'd never have let you actually marry her." She gave a snort. "Chase and I made a pact about that."

"It's good to know you both had my back." Logan laughed. "But for the record, I'd never have actually married her." He shook his head. "When I learned that Hazel had asked Chase to the premier, I didn't want to go. But then my mother told me to ask Melissa. She said that it would help her career to have her name attached to ours."

"Isn't her father some big movie exec?" Rose said.

"Yes, he is. They own the Shaw Television Network." Logan rubbed his hip, which was starting to ache. "But he couldn't just make a show or made for TV movie for his daughter." He cleared his throat. "He has partners and an entire board to answer to."

"Tell him," Logan heard Chase say to Rose.

"No!" Rose hissed at him. "Now is not the time."

"Not the time to tell me what?" Logan frowned.

"See what you've done now?" Rose moaned at Chase. "It's nothing, Logan. Really and I probably didn't hear what was being said correctly."

"Not *that*!" Chase rasped. "The *other* thing. You know when Melissa threatened you."

"Melissa threatened you, Rose?" Logan felt little shock waves zap through his nerves.

"It was nothing," Rose brushed it off. "We were young, and she thought I had a crush on you."

"What?" Logan spat. "We all know that's not true, was it?"

"No, you pompous jackass!" Rose said indignantly. "You and Chase are like brothers to me."

"That's what I thought," Logan confirmed. "But why didn't you tell me Melissa threatened you, and when did she do that?"

"A few days before the premiere, she saw me leaving your house. Melissa pulled me aside to tell me in no uncertain terms that she would be the *only* woman in your life," Rose shocked him by saying. "Then went on to tell me to leave you alone permanently."

"Rose told her that the two of you had been friends since before you could walk, and you would be friends until you were old and in a nursing home together." Chase laughed.

"I"m sorry, Rose," Logan blew out a breath. "I can't believe I let myself be tied to her for so long."

"Like you said, she was safe," Rose pointed out. "And your mother needed to keep the two of you together."

"What's that supposed to mean?" Logan's brows knit tightly together as alarm bells went off in his head.

"Melissa's father was blackmailing your mother," Chase blurted out. "That's why she pushed you to go to the premier with Melissa in the first place."

"No." Logan refused to believe that was true. "What could he possibly have on my mother or father? They are squeaky clean."

"You know, for an intelligent guy, you are so naive!" Chase's voice was tinged with frustration. "Trust me, no one in that business is *squeaky* clean, and I should know I'm a publicist to some of the top celebrities." He went quiet for a few seconds. "If you like, I can try and find out what I can about your parents."

"Rose, tell me what you overheard and when," Logan pushed Chase's offer aside for the moment.

Another silence fell over the other side of the phone, and he could picture Rose scratching her head as she did when she didn't want to tell you something.

"Do you want me to tell him?" Chase asked Rose.

"No!" Rose said emphatically. "The night of your farewell party seven years ago, I went to your room to use your bathroom." She paused. "When I was leaving, I heard angry voices from the guest bedroom next to yours."

"At first, Rose thought it was your mother and father arguing," Chase picked up the story. "But as she was sneaking away, she heard the man say that he believes Logan has been seeing a local girl and gave your mother photographic proof."

Logan's eyes widened as it dawned on him that it hadn't been his parents that were having him followed — it was the Shaws.

"It was Melissa's father. He told your mother in no uncertain terms to fix the problem and get you and Melissa back together," Rose continued from where Chase had left off. "He went on to remind your mother to remember the deal, and as long as she held up her side of it, your mother's secret was safe."

"What secret?" Logan's brow was knit tightly together, and he could feel a tension headache starting to pound behind his eyes.

Logan felt like he'd stepped into some weird alternate reality. Where his life wasn't the neatly ordered one he thought it was but a shambles of lies, secrets, and betrayal.

"I don't know," Rose answered him. "All I heard after that was your mother saying she'd deal with the problem."

"Deal with the problem?" Logan couldn't believe what he was hearing.

Maybe Rose was right, and she didn't overhear the conversation correctly. But he knew he was grasping at straws. Rose had excellent hearing and an eerie ability to know whose footsteps were coming behind them. She never forgot a voice or face.

"I wish I had, Logan," Rose's voice dropped.

"Oh, my word!" Chase breathed angrily. "Was my sister the problem your mother was going to deal with?"

"I...." Logan's mind was reeling as Melissa's words from earlier that day came back to haunt him. *Don't pretend you didn't know how your mother helped you get out of that mess with Chase's little sister all those years ago.* "I'm not sure."

"You're not sure?" Chase hissed. "What happened that night?" There was a pause, and Chase continued before Logan could say anything. "That's why my sister left without any explanation the day after your party."

"Chase thought Hope was eager to get back to her boyfriend she'd had at college in Boston," Rose added.

"I don't know what happened that night," Logan told them honestly. "I had to try and keep my distance from Hope. I didn't want it getting out about us until we were both ready or until after we met the following morning."

"The following morning?" Rose asked.

"Yes. I was planning on proposing to Hope on the pier. It was our favorite meeting spot and where we shared our first kiss," Logan cleared his throat as the old familiar ache throbbed through his heart when he thought of that summer. "I had been kept busy at the party with people wanting to wish me well." He rubbed the back of his neck, and when I eventually got a chance to sneak away, I couldn't find Hope."

"Was it around eleven?" Chase asked.

"I think so," Logan nodded.

"She'd gone back to Boston by then," Rose told him.

"I know," Logan's voice caught at the memory. "I found Marli, and she wasn't very friendly."

"I can imagine," Rose said. "Especially if she thought you'd hurt Hope."

"Wait!" Logan breathed, his eyes opening wide. "Marli would've known who Sydney's father was."

"Don't remind me of how my family lied to me," Chase hissed.

"Yes, I know how that feels!" Logan ran his hand through his hair. "While I know you're hurt about them keeping Sydney's father's identity from you...." His voice trailed off. "Until you discover the secret they kept from you is a child that no one told you about." He cleared his throat. "And suddenly, your whole world is out of balance, and you start redefining who you are because you are no longer just you. You're a dad."

"I guess it was worse for you," Chase relented. "And I apologize for not staying to support you. I saw the shock on your face when Thorn confirmed you were Sydney's father."

"It's okay," Logan told Chase. "I can understand what a shock it must've been for you too." He sighed. "I'm sorry I didn't tell you about Hope, Chase. That was wrong of me." He wet his lips and put his head back against the wall. "It's no excuse, but I was hurting, and I think I've never gotten over Hope. When you spoke about her or Sydney, it was like the wound in my heart was ripped apart."

"You really loved my sister that much?" Chase asked softly.

"I did...." Logan swallowed. That was a lie. "I do!"

"Well, then, buddy," Chase said. "You need to talk to her."

"I know," Logan agreed. "And I will. But now doesn't seem like the best time."

"It never is the best time!" Rose told him. "Trust me. You just need to make it the perfect time."

"Did you never suspect you were Sydney's father?" Chase asked him.

"I did when you first told me Hope was four months pregnant," Logan told Chase. "But then you said the father was Hope's boyfriend from college." He rubbed his thigh. "I still had a nagging feeling the baby may be mine, so I called Marli and...." He frowned as his words trailed off.

"What did Marli say?" Rose and Chase said simultaneously.

"I asked her if it was true that Hope was pregnant and the baby's father had left her," Logan repeated his conversation with Marli. "Her exact words to me were, yes, that's true, the baby's father had left Hope alone and heartbroken."

"That's not confirming what Chase said," Rose pointed out. "That was Marli throwing you a big hint."

"I realize that now!" Logan hissed. "Good grief, what an idiot I've been." He shook his head. "My grandparent's house is full of pictures of Sydney, and they always told me how much she reminded them of me at that age."

"Well, that's not a big hint!" Chase said sarcastically. "How did you not know she was yours?" He said in disbelief. "Even with all the misunderstandings, some part of you must've known."

"Maybe subconsciously," Logan admitted. "But mostly, I felt they were rubbing salt into my still raw Hope wound." He defended his actions.

"So you didn't want to know!" Chase's voice was laced with angry accusations. "You preferred to hide away with Melissa."

"You have no idea what I feel, Chase," Logan's own anger sparked. "If you ever find out you have a secret baby, then you come back and tell me that deep down you knew!"

"I'm not as careless as you, buddy," Chase sneered. "And I would step up and find out for definite if the child was mine before slinking into a safe space to nurse my wounded ego."

"Chase!" Rose shouted at him. "What the heck is wrong with you?"

"It's okay, Rose," Logan said with a sigh. "He has every right to be angry with me, and maybe he's right. I did run away because I didn't want to risk further hurt or humiliation."

"I'm sorry our families kept this from you," Chase told Logan. "Thank you for being honest about you and Hope. If you really love her, and she loves you, then I couldn't ask for a better person for her to be with." He went quiet for a few minutes. "But Logan, you must make this right with Hope and Sydney and rid yourself of Melissa once and for all."

"I'm way ahead of you on the Melissa front," Logan assured him. "And thank you, Chase."

"Now, do you want me to look into your parents and Melissa's?" Chase asked.

"I guess so," Logan accepted his help. "I'd better get back to Sydney."

"Oh, and the barbecue is back on, but it's being moved to my house," Rose informed him. "Chase and I have already messaged everyone he invited."

"Great!" Logan nodded, pushing himself up and exercising his aching leg and hip.

They said goodbye after briefly talking about the barbecue. Logan was returning to Sydney's room when Hope stopped him.

"Logan, would you come with me to get some clothes for Sydney at my apartment?" Hope asked him.

"Sure," Logan agreed.

"Good." Hope looked nervous. "And... uh... I thought we could talk along the way."

CHAPTER FIFTEEN

Hope and Logan didn't say much as they walked to Hope's car. On the drive to her apartment, they spoke about Sydney's operation and when she'd be released from the hospital. Hope and Logan fell into an awkward silence during the last few minutes of the journey.

Say something about Sydney's father. Hope's mind whirled as she tried to find the words.

But how do you tell someone they're your child's father? Although after the events at the hospital, Hope was more than sure he already had a hunch. Her heart twinged, thinking about how Logan must be feeling.

Could it be possible he hasn't put the pieces together? Hope stole a glance at Logan.

He was staring out the side window. He didn't seem tense, but when it came to Logan, Hope wasn't good at reading him. The last time she'd thought she knew what he was feeling, she'd had her heart broken. This time there was a lot more at stake than her heart. This was about Sydney, and Hope wouldn't rely on her feelings when it involved her daughter's happiness.

"Have you heard more from Bradley about the notes and

us being spied on?" Logan asked, pulling her from her thoughts as they neared the bakery.

"No, I haven't," Hope told him. "I tried to contact him earlier, but his phone kept going to voicemail. That was right before I got my mother's messages about Sydney, and I haven't tried since."

"Oh, did you find out more information?" Logan looked at her inquiringly.

"Yes, you were going to be my next call after Bradley, but then I had to rush to the hospital," Hope explained.

She glanced at Logan. Their eyes met briefly, and Hope's heart lurched again at the flicker of emotion she saw in them. She clenched her hands tightly on the steering wheel to stop them from shaking as the realization that Logan knew the truth hit her.

"What did you find out?" Logan asked curiously.

Hope was glad for the distraction, and she told him about her meeting with Lance, James Grant, and finding out who may have written the threatening letters to her.

"No way!" Logan looked at her in disbelief. "Gloria Williams wrote those notes?"

"Yes, and there's more." Hope swallowed. She was about to give him two big surprises tonight. "I found out who installed the surveillance equipment in my building."

"Let me guess." Logan turned to her, holding up his hand. "Melissa Shaw."

"What?" Hope's face crinkled at the mention of that woman's name. The woman who'd come between her and her first big love. "No, why on earth would she...." Her eyes widened. "Is she the one that had you followed?"

"We'll get there," Logan promised. "First, finish your story."

"Winston Manning!" Hope looked at Logan. His eyes widened in surprise.

"My grandparent's estate manager, Winston Manning?"

Logan said, stunned. "That must be a mistake. Winston would never...."

Hope looked at him when his words trailed off and saw his jaw clench.

"What is it?" Hope's eyes widened questioningly.

"Winston is Gloria Williams's older brother," Logan said through gritted teeth.

"So it is her threatening and spying on me—" Hope corrected herself. "Us."

"It doesn't make any sense," Logan said, exasperated. "Why would Gloria Williams want to spy on us and warn you away from me?"

"I can't answer that. At least not yet," Hope told him. "But I know how a note Bradley took from my office this morning got delivered."

"You know about that?" Logan asked guiltily.

"I think the better question is, how do you know about that?" Hope looked at him accusingly.

"Bradley showed it to me this morning when he gave me a lift home," Logan confessed. "I was going to tell you earlier today, but...." He cleared his throat and shifted uncomfortably in the seat. "Um....I had to leave."

"Oh!" Hope looked at him curiously. "That's what you wanted to talk about after my dip in the duck pond."

Logan laughed softly at her reference to Barbie pushing Hope into the pond. "Yes, that was part of what I wanted to talk to you about." He cleared his throat. "But before we get into the second part, you were telling me about how the note got delivered to your desk."

"Yes, Jane Iverson, she's been working for me since I expanded the business to catering and event planning," Hope explained.

They turned onto Main Road and drove through the center of town.

"I know Jane," Logan told her. "We always thought she was the one that would go on to be a champion figure skater."

"So did she," Hope said. "But it turns out that Tiffany tampered with two of her top competition skates at one of the championships and blamed it on Jane. Worse, she got it on video. Jane said it couldn't have been her because she'd gotten food poisoning and wasn't even at the rink that day."

"So, Tiffany blackmailed Jane into forfeiting," Logan guessed. "I remember that competition because everyone was shocked when Jane retired from skating for no reason."

"I thought it was strange that someone with Jane's cooking skills would pack in a top position at one of the best restaurants in New York to come work for me," Hope told Logan. "But Jane said she couldn't take the stress and had started to hate cooking. She convinced me she wanted to slow down and enjoy what she did again."

"Tiffany blackmailed Jane into quitting her job by getting hired at your bakery?" Logan shook his head. "But Jane doesn't skate anymore, so why would she worry about a competition that happened so long ago. She can't be charged for it."

"No, Tiffany's now blackmailing her with attempted murder," Hope told him.

Hope saw Logan's eyes widen. "Who did Jane try to murder?"

"Tiffany!" Hope shocked Logan by saying. "She has a video of Jane pushing Tiffany into the street when the motorbike hit her." She shook her head, thinking of how scared Jane must be to have agreed to do what Tiffany made her do. "The thing is that Jane was with Tiffany when she was pushed into the road."

"Did Jane not see who pushed Tiffany?" Logan gaped at the information.

"She didn't say because even though she's come clean with me, Jane has a four-year-old daughter," Hope told Logan. "And she's already caused waves by telling Gloria and Tiffany that she will no longer be their spy. Jane admitted that she enjoyed working for me as she was starting to burn out in New York."

"So, Jane agreed to take the job at your bakery to protect her daughter?" Logan guessed.

"Yes." Hope nodded. "Lance wants her to continue to work for them. But she'd be pretending to spy on me when she's really spying on them. He wants Jane to try to get the video evidence they have on her."

"But didn't you say she wrote back to Gloria telling her she would no longer spy for her?" Logan looked at Hope.

Hope pulled into her driveway and switched off her engine then opened her car door.

"Yes, but James didn't deliver the note. He dropped it, and that is how I learned about Jane," Hope told him.

"So, James either doesn't want Jane to get into trouble with the Williams family, or he's trying to protect you!" Logan pointed out.

"Or both!" Hope suggested, climbing out the car. "Should we continue this inside? I'm dying for a decent cup of coffee."

Logan nodded, getting out of the car, and as they walked to the door, Hope stopped, frowning, as she noticed it was ajar and the lights were on.

"That's strange," Hope said and was about to push the door open when Logan stopped her.

"No, don't!" Logan maneuvered around her and listened at the door.

"It was probably Thorn or one of his kids not pulling the door closed properly when they came to get Barbie," Hope reasoned.

"It doesn't hurt to be cautious," Logan said, slowly pushing the door open and stepping inside.

Hope followed him. The feeling of unease that had come and gone the whole day was back with a vengeance. Hope was amazed at how silently Logan managed to move even with his limp and cane. They stopped at the door to the bakery kitchen. It was open, and the lights were on. Logan stepped inside, and she heard him draw in a breath. Wanting to see what had shocked him, Hope stepped around him and froze, her breath catching in her throat.

"Oh no!" Hope's eyes widened, and her heart hammered as she let out the breath she'd held.

The kitchen had been vandalized. Items that were on the shelves were strewn all over the floor. The pastry fridge's door was open, and all the cupcakes, tarts, muffins, cakes, and other baked goods had been destroyed.

"Hope!" Logan called out to her.

She turned toward the sound of his voice. Hope had been so stunned by the sight of her kitchen she hadn't realized that Logan had gone to check the rest of the store. He was standing in her office. A whooshing sound rose in her head, and she felt like she was walking in a dream state as she went to her office. Hope now understood the meaning of a room being tossed. Her desk drawers were left open, and papers were strewn everywhere. Her monitor had been smashed, and her keyboard was lying in pieces on the floor.

"Why would anyone do this?" Hope felt the sting of tears burn her eyes as her voice grew hoarse with emotion.

"Maybe that's why!" Logan pointed to some writing on the wall that Hope hadn't even noticed through the haze of shock resounding through her body.

You were warned! It was scrawled in what looked like lipstick.

"Is that paint?" Logan walked closer to the writing.

"No, it looks more like Dior Rouge lipstick," Hope said.

"That's rather specific." Logan frowned and turned to her as she bent in front of the wall and picked something up. "You can tell what color and make it is just by looking at it?"

"No, because whoever wrote that on the wall left this." Hope showed him the lipstick she'd picked up.

"I take it that's not yours?" Logan guessed.

"I would never buy a lipstick that expensive," Hope told him, and she saw him frown.

"You shouldn't have picked it up," Logan told her, stepping closer to look at the item, and she saw recognition flash in his eyes.

"Do you know whose lipstick this is?" her brow creased as she looked at him accusingly.

"I'm not sure," Logan told her. "I think you should put it back where you found it." He suggested. "This is a crime scene."

Hope nodded and put the lipstick back where she found it and saw Logan pull his phone out of his jeans pocket.

"Who are you calling?" Hope asked him.

"Lance," Logan told her. "I'm not sure I trust the Bar Harbor police. Especially if you think Gloria Williams is involved."

"Why?" Hope looked at him quizzically.

"Because, according to my grandmother, Gloria Williams is dating the police captain." Logan's words took her by surprise.

"Oh!" Hope's eyes widened.

"He's not answering," Logan said softly before leaving a voice message for Lance. "I've checked the shop, and it wasn't vandalized."

"Then whatever they were looking for was in here," Hope guessed, and her eyes widened. "What if it was the vagrant burglar?"

"You said yourself, other than a few bakery antiques and an old cash register, you had nothing of value that the vagrant burglar would want," Logan reminded her.

"What about Marli's place?" Hope paled, and she dashed out of the office back into the kitchen, going to the large double doors that led to Marli's kitchen next door. "Oh, thank goodness it's still locked."

"I think we should check your apartment," Logan said.

Hope nodded and followed him up the stairs. The door to her apartment was open, but no lights were on. Hope was about to switch the hall light on, but Logan grabbed her hand, stopping her and making her heart flip-flop in her chest from his touch.

"No, don't," Logan whispered.

His hand lingered on hers for longer than necessary before he pulled it away and turned his phone light on. They checked out the kitchen first, and it looked like it had been untouched before they made their way to the living room. Hope and Logan were about to enter the room when a figure dressed entirely in black pushed past them. Logan was knocked into Hope, who slammed into the wall behind her hitting her head and making her see stars.

"Hope!" Logan immediately staggered off her, battling to steady himself without his cane. "Speak to me." He said, frantically trying to see if she was hurt in the faint light of his phone that had fallen on the floor cast in the hallway.

"I'm fine," Hope moaned, rubbing her aching head. "Who on earth was that?"

"I'm sorry," Logan's voice was filled with regret and frustration. "If I could, I'd go after her."

"You can't." Red-hot anger at her home and business being ransacked spurted through her. "But I can."

Before Logan could stop her, she pushed past him and rushed down the stairs ignoring the sick feeling in her stomach, lightheadedness, and pain throbbing at the back of her head.

"Hope!" Logan yelled after her, but she ignored him.

Hope rounded the corner at the bottom of the stairs trying to remember if she had closed the side entrance door to the building or not when they came in. She rounded the corner from the stairs and saw that the side door was wide open.

"Shoot!" Hope hissed, having wanted to catch the burglar inside rather than have to rush into the dark streets after them.

She flew through the side door and collided with a wall of muscle.

"What the…." Hope bounced backward from the collision feeling even more lightheaded and tripped over the steps but was caught by a strong pair of arms.

"I've got you!" Lance's welcome voice sounded like music to her ears.

"And I've got her." The wall of muscle was James Grant, holding a frantically wiggling woman dressed in black from head to toe. She even had black latex gloves on.

"Lance!" Logan's voice had them all turning toward the side door.

His eyes slit, moving over Hope and Lance, who was still holding onto her. Guilt ripped through her, and she quickly stepped away from Lance.

"Hey, Logan," Lance greeted him. "I got your message and came as soon as we could."

"I know you," Logan said to James. "You work for Crow Security."

"No, I used to work for them," James's eyes narrowed before he and Lance exchanged a look. "I work for Glory Security now."

James looked at the woman who'd stilled in his arms when she heard Logan's voice. That's when Hope recognized the woman's perfume, and her anger erupted once again.

"I see you caught the person who vandalized my bakery and home!" Hope said through gritted teeth.

"We caught her and her accomplices," Lance told Hope. "I'm sorry we didn't get here sooner but we were saving Bradley from drowning in the river."

He pointed to the black SUV parked behind Hope's car, and Bradley waved from the window.

“What?” Hope’s eyes widened.

“I think you should ask his fiance’s ex that question,” Lance suggested, looking at the woman who’d gone completely still, her eyes sending daggers Hope’s way.

“Hardy Bryant tried to drown Bradley?” Logan’s frown deepened.

“Nope, not Hardy,” Lance answered and opened the back door of his car. He pulled a tall, distinguished-looking man from the vehicle, making Hope suck in her breath. “He and his niece tried to drown Bradley.”

“Winston?” Hope breathed. “Why....” Her voice trailed off in confusion, and she looked at Logan, who was staring at the man in shock.

“That’s not Winston,” Logan said, shaking his head.

“What?” Hope looked at Logan as if he’d gone mad. “Then who is he?”

“I don’t know,” Logan shook his head, staring at the man. “But it’s *not* Winston.”

“But there’s no denying this—” Hope hooked the bottom of the woman in black’s balaclava and yanked it off her head. “Is none other than America’s not so sweetheart.” She tossed the balaclava onto the hood of Lance’s car. “Hello, Melissa.”

Hope raised an eyebrow as she faced the woman who had been a thorn in her side for longer than she cared to remember. The woman that had come between her and the only man she’d ever loved. Hope’s eyes widened at realizing she was still in love with Logan. She turned to see Logan staring angrily at Melissa.

“Let go of me, you brute!” Now that she’d been exposed, she struggled against the beefy hands clamped around her upper arms, holding her captive. Her eyes narrowed to malicious slits as she glared at Hope. “Where did you hide it?”

“Hide what?” Hope frowned at her

“Don’t act innocent with me!” Melissa spat. “I know it

was you that took it." She tried to yank herself out of James's grip to step forward, but he held her steady.

"What are you talking about, Melissa?" Logan hissed at her.

"My flash drive!" Melissa eyed him angrily. "She broke into my house and stole personal information."

"What?" Hope spluttered. "I have never broken into anything in my entire life."

"I have evidence to prove otherwise," Melissa challenged. "My security system caught you on camera taking the drive."

"I don't even know where you live." Hope looked at her, getting angrier and angrier at Melissa, who was clearly trying to frame her for something. "But you're going to pay for breaking, entering, and vandalizing because I'm pressing charges."

"Go ahead!" Melissa sneered, looking down her nose at Hope. "You'll end up doing time for breaking into my house and stealing personal information." Her lip curled nastily. "Who do you think the court's going to believe?" She gave a cruel laugh. "Me or some little baker who had an affair with my fiance behind my back and then tried to trap him with a secret child breaking my heart?"

"Melissa!" Logan hissed warningly. "That's enough."

Hope saw red dots flash before her eyes as her anger boiled over, and she had to curl her hands into tight fists to stop herself from slapping Melissa.

"Are you talking about this?" Jane walked up the driveway holding a red and black flash drive. "I got it hand-delivered to me late this afternoon."

"You!" Melissa hissed. "Give that back to me."

She kicked her heel into James's shin, making him wince, and as his grip loosened, Melissa broke free and lunged at Jane, who sidestepped her attack while James caught the actress.

"Did you get Tiffany?" Jane asked Lance, who nodded as

she handed him the disk. "I think you'll find many interesting things on that disk. Including the real images of Melissa pushing Tiffany into the road."

"No one will believe you or that footage," Melissa told them. "I will say they're fake, and you're trying to ruin my reputation because you're friends with her." She nodded toward Hope.

"I think you should stop talking now, Melissa," the Winston double said in clipped tones.

"Who are you?" Logan asked the tall man.

"I'm the Shaw's attorney and fixer." The man's cold eyes stared at Logan. "Although I also work for my niece, Tiffany Williams, occasionally." His gaze never wavered, nor did his calm tone falter as he introduced himself to Logan. "I'm Quinten Manning. I believe my twin brother, Winston, works for your grandfather."

CHAPTER SIXTEEN

Logan stood staring at Quintin Manning in disbelief. The man looked like Winston, but Winston had a professional air about him, and he was kind and warm. Quintin was the exact opposite of kind and friendly. The man looked like a stone statue.

Logan could understand why the Shaws would have an attorney. Everyone had an attorney these days, but what would they need a fixer for? And why would Quintin disclose he was one? And when he'd introduced himself and who he was, he'd specifically addressed Logan.

He gave himself a mental shake. The bizarre happenings of the past few days were making him paranoid. Logan had also stopped taking his pain medication and had a constant burning ache running down the damaged side of his body. The pain was probably messing with his mind as well.

"Quintin, you'd better get that drive back," Melissa's angry voice pulled Logan from his thoughts. "I'm not the only one that disk has *personal* information on."

Her eyes met and held Logan's as a smug smile split her lips.

"What is this all about, Melissa?" Logan asked her. His voice was void of emotion.

"You!" Melissa spat. "Don't you get it?" Her eyes narrowed. "It's always been about you!"

"Me?" Logan looked at her in shock. "You're not in front of your doting fans now, Melissa." He looked around and took a step closer to Hope, who turned and gave him a tight smile. "You can drop the adoring girlfriend act now. We all know the only person Melissa Shaw cares about is herself and being a superstar."

"Yes, I wanted to be a superstar," Melissa hissed. "I grew up watching the beautiful Felicia Burns enchant audiences worldwide with her acting skills." Her eyes narrowed. "I knew I wanted to be Felicia Burns, and I was determined to get on the *Trouble with Daisy* show no matter what it took."

"And what did it take, Melissa?" Logan looked at her with disgust. "Blackmail?"

"Whatever it took!" Melissa's eyes were hooded as she gave him a smug smile answering vaguely. "I didn't get the part I wanted no matter how much money my father tried to invest in the show."

"Melissa!" Quintin hissed at her warningly. "I'd really stop talking if I was you."

"Oh, please, Quintin," Melissa brushed him off arrogantly. "What are they going to do? We both know my father will have me out of here before I even get to the police station." She laughed. "That's if the police even come at all."

"Oh, they're coming to take you away," Hope assured her and looked at Logan. "You see, this is why I've never wanted Sydney caught in the undertow of the craziness of show business. I can't stand how celebrities think they are above everything, even the law."

Logan was taken aback by the venom in Hope's voice. "Not all celebrities are spoiled like Melissa." He defended his family. "My grandparents are still celebrities who went above and beyond to respect your wishes. To the point of lying to my parents and me."

Logan couldn't help the anger and hurt still simmering over finding out the truth about Sydney. A truth Hope had yet to talk to him about. Although he had a feeling that is why she'd asked him to accompany him, and he hoped they would still be able to.

"I know!" Hope snapped back at him. "I know what your grandparents did for me to protect Sydney. But they weren't lying to you. You never bothered to ask them about Sydney." Her eyes narrowed angrily at him. "Did you ever wonder why their house is practically a shrine to her?"

"No, I tried not to think about it." Logan's temper started to rise.

As it did, the emotional bubble he'd trapped his hurt, confusion, and anger from never getting closure from Hope finally burst.

"Of course, you wouldn't want to *think* about it," Hope rasped. "Because this is one *mess* your mommy wouldn't be able to clear up for you!"

Her words felt like a slap across his face as the conversation with Rose and Chase about his farewell party seven years ago rang through his mind. *Your mother said she'd fixed the problem.* He swallowed as his head shot up, and his eyes clashed with Melissa's, who had a smug look on her face. Her words rang through his mind. *Don't pretend you didn't know your mother got you out of a mess with Chase's little sister.*

Logan felt as if someone had put their hand through his chest and was squeezing his heart as another conversation he'd had that night seven years ago blistered his conscious.

Why do you want to find Hope? Do you want to ensure your mommy did your dirty work for you? Marli had snarled at him.

Now Marli's words made sense to him. Logan took a deep

breath, his fists clenched at his sides, as he forced his anger into check. He'd been so on edge about Sydney, being watched, and the burglary at Hope's place that he'd let his emotions get the better when Hope aimed her anger at him. Logan looked at all the eyes, watching them intently and frowning when he noticed Gloria Williams and her youngest daughter Mindy standing, staring at them.

When did they get here? Logan wondered. Hope and he had been so fired up he hadn't heard them arrive. *Why were they here?*

"Uh....is this a bad time?" Gloria Williams looked from Logan to Hope. "We don't mean to intrude, but my brother called us and told us to meet him here."

Logan watched Gloria frown as her eyes landed on Quintin and then drifted to Melissa.

"Where is Winston?" Gloria asked, trying to see into the bakery.

"Winston?" Logan asked. "He isn't here. Why did you think he would be?"

"Because he called me and told me to meet him here," Gloria told Logan. "Mindy and I were buying groceries and stopped here to meet him on our way home."

"He's not here." Hope's eyes narrowed as she looked at Gloria.

"H—hel—lo, Hope," Mindy, who went to school with Hope and was a mousy, timid girl with a bad stutter, stammered and smiled at her.

"Hello, Mindy," Hope's voice softened. "I'm sorry you had to witness our fight." She glared at Logan. "But tensions are running high here this evening after the break-in."

"B—b—break-in?" Mindy's eyes widened behind her thick, dark, framed glasses that did nothing for her pretty amber eyes.

"Yes." Hope's angry eyes settled on Melissa. "Seem's America's Sweetheart is actually America's lying heart."

"Oh!" Mindy snorted at Hope's words and giggled. "Y—yess. Me—M—Melissa has never b—b—b—b—been k—k—k—ind."

"Oh, what do you know, you little freak!" Melissa said nastily. "You hide away doing what you do at your computer all day?"

"Acc—ccc—ounting," Mindy stepped closer to Hope, bowing her head slightly at Melissa's attack.

"Leave my daughter alone," Gloria's frosty tones snapped through the air. "I think you've done quite enough leading my eldest daughter astray and getting her into endless trouble." She looked at Quintin in disgust. "I see you're here to mop up your client's mess as usual."

"Clients who helped keep you and your other daughter out of jail, if I remember correctly," Quintin drawled.

Logan watched Gloria's face pale, and a warning look flashed in her eyes as she glared at Quintin. Logan's brows furrowed as he wondered why Quintin would divulge something like that to a crowd of practical strangers. Quintin was an attorney, and Logan may not be an expert on the law, but he did know Quintin must've broken some rules by divulging them. His brow knitted tighter together as he couldn't quite shake the feeling there was a lot more to Quintin Manning, and he was trying to tell them something.

"I think we should take the culprits to the station," Lance interrupted, looking at his wristwatch. "We can't wait here much longer. I have to call the police to the crime scene."

"You haven't called the police yet?" Hope hissed at Lance and pulled her phone from her pocket. "I'll do it."

"No, wait!" Winston's voice had them spinning around to see him rushing up the driveway with Tiffany Williams in tow. "Sorry I took so long to get here, but my niece can be rather elusive when she's in trouble."

"Why would I be in trouble?" Tiffany demanded. "It was all her idea." She pointed to Melissa.

"I'd be very careful pointing fingers, Tiffany," Melissa warned her icily. "Just remember there's always three pointing back at you when you do."

"Is that another threat, Melissa?" Tiffany's eyes sparked with anger. "I told you this would happen if you pushed things." She snarled. "But no, your wayward way of life forced us into this position."

"Shut up, Tiffany!" Melissa said through clenched teeth. "I can still ruin your family."

"No, my dear, I'm afraid you can't," Winston drawled. "You see, I had a heart-to-heart with my niece on the way here. I also have a copy of that flash drive your mother gave me and had a copy sent to Jane."

"My mother?" Melissa spluttered. "When did she get back to town?"

"Oh, she's been here for a few months," Winston told Tiffany.

"Does my father know?" Melissa turned to Quintin. "You'd better start dialing him right now. You know he's been looking for my mother for months now."

"I'm afraid I can't do that," Quintin told her, stepping towards his brother, Winston.

"What do you mean?" Melissa hissed. "You work for my father and me. You're *our fixer* now fix this and call my father."

"Melissa, your father is not going to save you this time," Winston told her. "He's in hot water himself and has been taken in by the FBI in California for money laundering and extortion."

"You're lying!" Melissa spat, her eyes narrowing dangerously on Winston.

"I'm afraid he's not lying." Lance stepped forward. "Do you know why he was after your mother?"

"Because she's a lying, cheating, thief who stole more than half of our fortune," Melissa snarled.

"No, Melissa." Lance shook his head. "Because your father was abusive and controlling, the money your mother took was her money. Not your father's, and she alerted Winston to how your father has been blackmailing the Halls and a few other celebrities."

"What was he blackmailing my family with?" Logan asked Winston.

"Maybe you should speak to your mother about this," Winston advised him.

"I can tell you!" Melissa looked at him with malice in her eyes. "You think my good girl American Sweetheart persona is false." She gave a crazy laugh. "Well, your mother is just as big a fraud."

"What is that supposed to mean?" Logan asked her angrily.

"That's enough, Melissa," Quintin warned her.

"What do you care?" Melissa turned on him. "You're supposed to be loyal to us and fix these things for my father."

"Melissa, I tried to keep you out of trouble," Quintin told her.

"Well, you get paid enough, yet here I am," Melissa sneered.

"I don't actually work for your father," Quintin confessed. "I work for your mother, and she hired me to keep an eye on you."

"You're working with my mother?" Melissa looked at him in disbelief. "She hates me."

"No, Melissa, your mother doesn't hate you," Quintin told her. "Your father poisoned you against her to punish her."

"Of course, you'd say that," Melissa looked at Lance. "Can you take me away, please?" Her eyes coldly looked at Hope and then at Logan. "I don't want to be around these toxic people."

"The police are on their way," James told Lance, who nodded. "Winston, will you bring Tiffany with you? I'll take

Quintin, Melissa, and Bradley with me." He stopped as he neared his car and frowned, looking around. "Where is Bradley?"

"I'm here," Bradley called as he slipped out of the bakery. "I was getting this all on film for Annabell and the Bar Harbor Daily."

"If you print this, my family will sue you!" Melissa warned him.

"No, they won't," Bradley told her. "Especially now that I know you and my...." He turned and glared at Tiffany. "Ex-fiance were plotting to kill me all because I uncovered why you're so desperate to get Logan to re-announce your engagement."

"I have dirt on you too, Bradley Danes!" Melissa reminded him.

"Oh, we have everything you and your father have been collecting on celebrities. And we know your father has been blackmailing them for years," Bradley informed her, his eyes narrowing as he turned and glared at Tiffany. "What did I ever do to you that would make you want to ruin my career as a correspondent like the two of you did?"

"You don't remember?" Tiffany looked at him in disbelief. "Yours and Annabell's expose on celebrity bullies?" Her voice started to shake with rage. "You ruined my career with that article you printed about me being the abuser and not the abused."

"I didn't write that article," Bradley told her. "It was before I knew your version of the truth. Which I, like a fool, fell for until I was anonymously sent that footage of what really happened between you and Hardy." His eyes widened. "Is that why you tried to have me killed?"

"Oh please, she doesn't have what it takes to have anyone killed!" Melissa looked at Tiffany in disgust. "She couldn't even do what needed to be done to win her first big competition."

"Melissa!" Quintin warned. "I may not agree with everything you've done. But I promised your mother, and right now, I won't be able to keep it if you incriminate yourself any more than you already have."

"Oh please." Melissa looked at everyone around her. "Who are my fans and the world going to believe?"

"How about this?" Bradley flipped his phone for her to see what he'd been recording.

"You can't do this!" Melissa tried to lunge forward to grab his phone, but this time, Quintin stopped her.

"Please, don't make things any worse than they already are for you." Quintin shook his head.

"You work for Melissa's mother?" Gloria looked at her brother in disbelief. "Since when?"

"Since I started working for the Shaw family," Quintin told her. "I'm sorry, little sister, but you must go with Winston and Tiffany to be debriefed by the FBI."

"Why me?" Gloria's eyes widened.

"Maybe because of the threatening notes you've been sending me and setting up illegal surveillance in my building!" Hope looked at her accusingly.

"What are you talking about?" Gloria asked her.

"The notes you've been leaving for me, warning me to stay away from the Halls and Logan in particular," Hope reminded her.

"Hope, I have no idea what you're talking about," Gloria looked at her indignantly. "Why on earth would I warn you away from the Halls or Logan?"

"I was going to ask you the same thing." Hope folded her arms and waited for her answer.

"Why would you even think it was me?" Gloria asked her, confused.

"Because your handwriting on your bakery order matches that of the notes," Hope told her.

“I don’t write my bakery order....” Gloria’s eyes widened, and she looked away from Hope for a second.

“Then who does?” Jane, Lance, Hope, and Logan asked at the same time.

“My uh....” Gloria swallowed nervously and cleared her throat. “My assistant, Gregory, does.”

“Gregory?” Lance frowned. “Gregory, who?”

“All my assistants details are at my house,” Gloria assured them. “I’m more than happy to give them to you.” She frowned and looked at Tiffany. “Did you drag Gregory into this mess?”

“No!” Tiffany shook her head. “I didn’t know Gregory was the one that was sending those notes for us.”

“Tiffany,” Melissa hissed again. “Shut up!”

“No, I’m sorry, Melissa. My uncle told me the authorities would be more lenient on me if I cooperated.” Tiffany turned and looked at Hope, Logan, and Lance. “I’ll tell you anything you want. I know I have to pay for what I’ve done, but all I ask is that I don’t have to do any time near....” She glared at Melissa. “Her.”

“All you’ve done?” Hope looked at Tiffany in shock.

“Look, Hope, I had nothing against you,” Tiffany assured her. “I’m sorry that we exposed your secret to....”

“Tiffany!” Melissa shouted. “Shut up!”

“You’ve exposed my secret?” Hope looked at her sideways. Her eyes widened with panic and fear. “What have you done, Tiffany?”

“I’m warning you.” Melissa glared at Tiffany.

“Oh shut up, Melissa,” Tiffany turned on her and then looked at Hope. “I’m sorry, Hope. You’ve always been nothing but kind to my sister and me.” She glanced at Mindy, her eyes filled with love.

“We sold your story to the press. And to authenticate it, we gave the press your daughter's birth certificate.” Melissa turned her malicious gaze toward Logan. "Along with the paternity test Logan ordered earlier today." Her eyes lit with satisfaction at seeing Hope's look of stunned horror. "Oh, you didn't know Logan had ordered one, did you?" She gave Logan a smug smile. "What do you think he was doing at the hospital when he ran into your mother and daughter?"

"Is this true?" Hope's eyes had turned dark with emotion.

"I...." Logan was so shocked that Melissa had somehow managed to intercept the test that he couldn't find the words, and all he blurted out was, "Yes."

The dark emotion in her eyes turned darker and shone with betrayal as she pursed her lips, nodded, then turned to Lance. "Please, can everyone leave?"

With that, Hope spun on her heel and rushed into the building.

"Hope, wait!" Logan called after her and was about to follow her but was stopped by Winston.

"No, let her go," Winston advised. He looked at Lance. "I'll wait here for the police." He looked at James and gave him his car keys. "Can you take my sister and Tiffany to Lance's office for questioning?"

"Sure." James nodded.

"Wh—wh—at about me?" Mindy looked to Winston for direction.

"Can you take your mother's car home?" Winston's voice softened, and his eyes warmed as he looked at his niece.

"I can," Mindy nodded. "If y—you don't want me to stay with you?"

"No, honey, I know you don't like crowds or being in tense situations." Winston smiled at her. "You go home."

Mindy nodded, taking the keys from her mother. She turned to look at Logan, "I—I'm sorry m—my sister caused this."

"Thanks, Mindy," Logan smiled at her.

Mindy took off her glasses to clean them on her shirt and smiled at him, nearly bowling him over as it transformed her face and made her beautiful amber eyes stand out. He saw something flash in them before she quickly put her glasses back on. Logan's brow creased as he looked at her.

"You have beautiful eyes," Logan complimented her. "Have you thought of wearing contacts?"

"I don't like touching my eyes," Mindy told him softly, stunning Logan further with her perfect diction. "Please tell Hope everything's going to be fine."

Logan's eyes widened, staring at her, stunned for a few seconds before Mindy shrunk into a shy mouse once again, saying goodbye and hurrying off. Logan stood staring after her, shaking his head, wondering if he'd imagined their exchange.

"Logan, are you ready to go?" Lance asked him, snapping him out of his thoughts.

"No," Logan said, shaking his head. "I'm going to stay."

"Logan..." Winston stepped up beside him.

"No, I have to," Logan told him. "I let her get away once before. I won't make the same mistake again."

"Fair enough, but I'm still staying too and I'll deal with the police," Wintson told him.

"We're going to leave you as I can hear the sirens," Lance told them as James ushered Tiffany and Gloria down the driveway to Winston's car.

Quintin started to usher Melissa toward Lance's SUV when Logan stopped them and walked up to Melissa.

"You never finished telling me why you did all this?" Logan looked at her questioningly. "Why would you want to ruin my life?"

"You have everything!" Melissa sneered. "A perfect family who dote on you and friends who would lay their lives down for you."

"You could've had all those things, too," Logan pointed out.

"Really?" Melissa looked at him and gave a mocking laugh. "My father didn't only control my mother. He controlled my life too, and I'd like to believe he stopped when I turned twenty-one, but the truth is it didn't. It just got even worse and that's why I was so eager to get married. To get away from him."

"So you did all this because you've got daddy issues?" Logan hissed.

"I did all this because I wanted your life!" Melissa's voice was raw with torment. "But you never saw me until my father arranged it with your mother."

"When I was sixteen." Logan clenched his jaw and shook his head. "Well, Melissa, my life wasn't that much different from yours."

"How so?" Melissa frowned.

"Because your father has inadvertently been controlling my life, too," Logan pointed out. "Although he did it differently, he pretty much dictated my life path."

Logan couldn't control the hurt and anger that reverberated in his voice. He saw Melissa's eyes widen in shock for the first time ever, and her features softened.

"I know this doesn't mean much." Melissa swallowed awkwardly. "But I'm sorry, Logan. I went crazy when I saw how you looked at Hope." She pursed her lips and let out a breath. "All I ever wanted was for you to look at me that way."

"So you had me and Hope followed and threatened because you were jealous?" Logan looked at her in disbelief.

"I didn't have you followed, nor did I threaten Hope," Melissa told him. "When you started dating Hope seven years ago, I got a message from someone named Super Fan."

"Super fan?" Logan's brow furrowed.

Melissa nodded. "Super Fan said they could help me get you back, but it would cost me."

"Cost you what?" Logan asked her.

"I had to get them information on certain people. And Super Fan sent me a special tablet I had to keep with me at all times to transfer the information on," Melissa told him.

"You were sent a tablet?" Lance looked at her questioningly. "That you uploaded files and—"

"Videos, pictures, recorded conversations." Melissa turned to Lance. "Whatever Super Fan wanted."

"And you kept this tablet on you at all times?" Quintin asked her, he too hadn't known about it.

"Yes," Melissa confirmed. "Well, most of the time."

"Where is it now?" Lance asked her.

"Super Fan contacted me this morning and told me they needed to upgrade it," Melissa explained. "Super Fan arranged a delivery service to come and box it up to take it away." She looked from Lance, to Quinting, and then Logan. "Super Fan is sending a new one that should arrive by tomorrow."

"So the tablet has already been collected?" Logan asked her.

"Yes." Melissa nodded. "But I made copies of everything I ever put on the tablet." She glanced to where Jane had been standing and frowned. "I'm sure that's the flash drive with all my backups that my mother sent to Jane."

"So it was Super Fan that's been watching us and threatening Hope?" Logan said.

"Yes," Melissa confirmed.

"Could Super Fan be Gregory, Gloria Williams, PA!" Logan said. "Hope said Gregory's handwriting matched the handwriting on the letters."

"I've never met Gregory," Melissa told them. "I had no idea Gloria had a PA."

"We'll find him," Lance assured Logan. "Now we'd better move."

"One more thing," Logan said, grabbing Melissa's arm. "What was your father blackmailing my mother about?"

"Your sister!" Melissa stunned Logan with the information before Quintin dragged her away and shoved her into the back of the SUV.

CHAPTER SEVENTEEN

Hope's mind was reeling, and her heart felt like it was hammering out of her chest as she shoved clothes into an overnight bag for Sydney. Her hands shook, and she felt physically ill at the thought of Sydney's paternity being splashed all over the news. Hope's stomach burned with anger when the word paternity popped into her head.

"How dare he?" Hope fumed, zipping up the bag and slinging it over her shoulder.

As she stormed out of Sydney's room, she wondered how Logan had gotten a sample of her DNA without Hope's permission. She walked into the living room to get Sydney's hair brush, and when she picked it up, she drew in a breath as realization dawned on her. The hairbrush was devoid of hair. A memory flashed through her mind of earlier that day. Logan had joked about the brush before he'd fled her apartment.

"Hope?" Logan walked cautiously into the room. "Can we—"

"You stole Sydney's hair?" Hope glowered, holding up the brush.

Logan held up his palms, stopping a few feet away from Hope. "If you'll let me explain."

"Explain?" Hope's brows raised as he looked at him in disbelief. "You came into our home and took something you had no right to take."

"No, right?" Logan's eyes flashed, and his shoulders stiffened. "You kept this secret from me for seven years, Hope." His voice was gruff with emotion. "Not only did you keep this from me, but you had my grandparents lie to me."

"They never lied to you, Logan," Hope's voice raised slightly. "You could've asked them any time on one of your super secret visits home." She shoved the hairbrush into a side pocket of the bag. "But if you're honest with yourself, Logan. You didn't want to know."

"That's not true," Logan declared. "I tried to find out if it was mine the minute I was told you were pregnant."

"I'm sure you did," Hope mocked, pushing past him.

"Can you just stop?" Logan grabbed her wrist, which she tried to yank away, but he tightened his grip. "You're not running away this time."

"Running away?" Hope's eyes blazed with anger, and her cheeks heated. "When did I *run* away?"

"The night of my farewell party," Logan accused. "You just took off without a word, and your cousin Marli told me in no uncertain terms to stay away from you."

"Maybe because she was protecting me from more humiliation when your mother warned me away," Hope exclaimed.

"What did my mother say to you, Hope?" Logan asked her, his eyes narrowing.

"Oh, don't act like you don't know." Hope glared at him. "All you had to do was say we were over and call it as it was." Her voice caught in her throat, and she desperately vied for control of her emotions, shocked to feel the power the memory still held over her. "A summer fling with your best friend's little sister."

"Is that what you think?" Logan's eyes darkened. He bit his bottom lip and nodded.

"What else was I supposed to think, Logan?" Hope's throat felt raw as the emotion was pulled from the depth of her soul. "One minute, you looked at me as if I was the only girl in the world, and the next, you were as cold as ice and aloof." She swallowed. She would not dissolve into a puddle of tears. "I saw Melissa call you when you stopped the car and got out on the way back to Bar Harbor from Bangor."

"That was not what you thought it was." Logan's voice was low and controlled. His eyes hooded.

"Really?" Hope breathed, unconvinced. "Well, what else was I supposed to think when you dropped me off, you couldn't wait to leave and broke all contact with me. Then you avoided me at the party, and I saw Melissa hanging onto you."

"If you looked closer, you would've seen me pushing her away and keeping her at arm's length as much as possible," Logan told her.

"Well, your mother was convinced the two of you were getting back together and couldn't wait to tell me the news of your engagement." Hope cleared her throat as her voice grew hoarse. She could feel the moisture build in her eyes. "She told me that you'd even bought the ring."

"What?" Logan hissed. "I had done no such thing!"

"Well, from where I was standing that night, it looked like everything your mother had said was true," Hope said, desperately swallowing down the lump in her throat.

"So, instead of speaking to me, you just ran away?" Logan accused.

"No, I did try and speak to you," Hope told him. "But I couldn't get your attention because you were otherwise occupied with Melissa."

"I told you I was keeping Melissa at arm's length, and if

we were standing together, it was to talk to a mutual acquaintance," Logan insisted.

"Oh, it was more than that, and you know it." Hope's frustration and anger spiked as she poked him in the chest with her index finger. "Melissa was playing the perfect hostess in her castle for everyone at the party to see."

"She was mingling like all celebrities do at parties," Logan defended.

"You can't help it, can you?" Hope accused. "Even now, after everything the superstar sweetheart has done, you rush to her defense."

"That's not what I'm doing," Logan stressed, his hand still gripping her wrist. His jaw clenched, and he pinched the bridge of his nose before taking a breath and looking at her. "You know, you could be right. I didn't really notice what Melissa was doing." He admitted. "My mind was in shambles and elsewhere most of the night. All I could think of was meeting you the next day."

"I saw just how shambled your mind was when I went to speak to you and ask you if it was true what your mother had said." Hope swallowed and cleared her throat as her voice caught. "But you were busily draped around Melissa, and from that kiss I witnessed, I knew I had my answer."

"Kiss?" Logan frowned and shook his head before his eyes widened in realization. "Why that scheming...." he said through gritted teeth. "Hope, that kiss was *not* what you thought it was. She kissed me, and I pushed her away, but I guess you didn't see that part."

"It looked exactly like I thought it was," Hope assured him. "After that, I couldn't stick around." She paused for a moment and gave a soft laugh. "You have no idea how that felt."

"I think I had some idea," Logan murmured.

"No, I don't think you do," Hope couldn't stop the tears that gathered in her eyes. As the memories were dredged up, she gave up trying to contain the hurt and betrayal that had lain unresolved for seven years. "You hurt me, Logan."

"Hope!" Logan looked stricken as he stared at her. "I...." He swallowed, his eyes darkening with emotion and his voice growing hoarse. "You hurt me, too."

"How did I hurt you?" Hope sniffed and swiped a stray tear from her cheek.

"You ran away into the night, leaving me without so much of a goodbye." Logan's voice caught in his throat, and he cleared it. His eyes locked with hers, and she sucked in a breath when he let her see the hurt festering in their depth. "I tried to find you, but Marli wouldn't tell me, and I couldn't ask Chase, although I did try in a roundabout way."

"You tried to find me?" Hope's brow furrowed as she looked at him and wiped away another tear.

"I did, I even called Marli a few times, but she wasn't very nice to me." Logan gave a small laugh. "Then, four months later, Chase told me you were pregnant, and when I asked him about the father, he said it was your college boyfriend."

"College boyfriend?" Hope looked at him in confusion. "Clint?" She gave her head a shake. "I'd broken off with him two months before the summer break when I was with you."

"I called Marli to confirm as I wanted so much for it...." Logan stopped and cleared his throat.

"So much to be what?" Hope's voice dropped, and her heart started to pound as she watched the emotion deepen in his eyes.

"So much for it to me," Logan admitted. "I wanted to be the father of your child."

Hope's heart filled to burst as her stomach knotted and her breath caught in her throat.

"I'm sorry, Logan," Hope whispered, gently pulling her wrist from his hand. "Can you wait here for a moment?"

Logan nodded and said teasingly, "You're not running away again, are you?"

"No!" Hope gave him a watery smile and left the room.

She rushed to her bedroom and dug in the back of her closet. Pulling out a photo album and journal, she returned to the living room where Logan was still standing where she'd left him. She stood a few feet away from him with the books in both hands.

"I wasn't trying to hide Sydney from you," Hope told him. "It's true I didn't want her caught up in your family's crazy fishbowl life." She looked at the books in her hand. "From the day I found out I was pregnant, I tried to write down what I would say when I told you." She turned the books in her hand, unable to meet his eyes. "You have no idea how often I started to call or message you." Hope looked up, and their eyes locked. "When Sydney was three months old, we visited Chase in California. He told me you were in town and convinced me to get a babysitter and attend a function your parents were hosting."

"You were in California with Sydney?" Logan's brows raised in surprise. "Why didn't you come to say hello?"

"I was going to," Hope told him. "But what Chase failed to tell me was that it was your official engagement party to Melissa that he'd brought me to."

"You were there that night?" Logan's eyes widened in despair. "If I'd known...."

"What would you have done?" Hope tilted her head slightly and smiled through the pain, squeezing her heart at the memory. "I made an excuse, and Chase got me a cab to his apartment." She swallowed and broke their eye contact to look at the books before holding them out to him. "So instead of writing actual letters, I started a journal—"

Logan walked forward and took the book, their fingers brushing and waking the butterflies in her stomach.

"What's in the journal?" Logan asked, holding it up but capturing her gaze.

"I started a journal for you," Hope's voice lowered. "At

first, I wrote in it nearly every night when I'd put Sydney to sleep." She worried her bottom lip with her teeth. "But then it whittled down to twice a week, and I've tried to write in it at least twice a month for the past six years."

Hope watched him as he went to open it and stopped him.

"Don't." Hope shook her head. "Don't read it now."

"Okay." Logan nodded and closed the book. "Can you tell what you wrote about?"

"I wrote all Sydney's milestones. Her first tooth, her first skinned knee, and when she learned to ride a bike," Hope told him. "I tried to fill the pages with as much of her life as I could so that one day when I finally got the chance to tell you, you'd have a journal of her life."

"Hope!" Logan's voice was hoarse, and his eyes sparkled with unshed tears. "Thank you."

"And this." Hope held up the photo album. "This is for you. I made sure I documented her life right up to the day you arrived home."

Logan took the album from her and wiped his eyes, "Can I look at the album at least?" He asked her.

"If you like," Hope said and glanced at her wristwatch. "But can you look at it in the car on the way to the hospital? I want to take Sydney's clothes to the hospital. I want to spend the night with her."

"Oh," Logan looked up at her. "Your mother and my grandmother said to tell you they want to spend the night with Sydney, and they've already passed it with the nursing staff."

"Oh!" Hope's face fell.

"But I'm sure you can spend the night as well," Logan told her quickly.

"No," Hope said. "As long as Sydney's happy with that. But I still want to go say goodnight to her."

"Would you mind if I tagged along?" Logan asked.

"No, I have to give you a lift home anyway." Hope laughed, pointing out that he didn't have a car.

"True." Logan grinned, walking toward her and taking the bag from her. He stopped in front of her. "I lied about something I did seven years ago."

Hope looked at him questioningly.

"I did get a ring." Logan's words hit her in the heart, but she bit down on the pain. "It was my great-grandmother's ring that I was having resized." His voice lowered even more. "But it wasn't for Melissa. It was for you." He swallowed, put the books beneath his arm, and reached into his jacket pocket, pulling out the blue velvet box. "I've kept this with me every day since I picked it up."

Logan handed her the box, and she looked at him wide-eyed as she popped it open and sucked in her breath. It was a square-cut emerald surrounded by diamonds with a white gold band.

"It's beautiful," Hope's eyes misted with tears as she closed the box. "This is why you were acting so strange that day we returned from Bangor?"

"Yeah." Logan nodded. "As soon as I knew the ring was ready, all I wanted to do was pull you into my arms and ask you to marry me." He gave a laugh. "But I had to distance myself to stop the impulse because I wanted it to be perfect."

"That's why you wanted to meet at the pier at sunrise that Sunday," Hope realized, her heart pounding in her chest.

"Yes." Logan nodded. "At our special place where we shared our first kiss."

"Oh, Logan." Hope handed him the ring back. "It seems our relationship wasn't doomed like I thought. It was sabotaged."

"Yes, and now I know why," Logan told her.

"Oh?" Hope looked at him curiously.

"I'll tell you on the way to the hospital," Logan promised,

and as they turned to leave, he stopped her. "I want to be a part of my daughter's life, Hope."

"I know," Hope said. "I want that, too."

"Which leaves the question of how and when do we tell her?" Logan asked.

"Why don't you come for dinner tomorrow night if they discharge her, and we'll talk to her together," Hope suggested.

"Okay," Logan agreed, and they started walking out the door and were stopped on the stairs by two detectives with Winston in tow.

"Hope Wright?" The one detective asked her, and she nodded. "Was anything vandalized or taken from upstairs?"

"No." Hope shook her head. "But Melissa was in the apartment when Logan and I came home."

"I see," the detective said. "Could you answer a few questions?"

"Can it wait?" Logan asked them. "We have to get to the hospital to see our daughter. We've already been delayed, and it's getting late."

"Sure," the detective said. "We'll be by tomorrow if that's okay with both of you."

"Okay," Hope said. "But could we come to the police station instead? Our daughter may come home tomorrow, and I don't want her upset by what happened here."

"That's fine," the detective handed her his card. "Just ask for me at the front desk."

Winston agreed to stay with the police while Logan and Hope went to the hospital. Hope was parking her car when she got a message. When she'd switched off the engine, she picked up her phone and frowned when she read it.

"Is everything okay?" Logan asked her.

"I'm not sure," Hope told him. "I have no idea who this is."

"Oh?" Logan looked at her curiously.

"It's from someone named Super Fan." Hope heard Logan

suck in a breath and looked up at him questioningly. "Do you know them?"

"No." Logan shook his head. "I know of them. What does the message say?"

"Don't worry, it's not your secret that will make the headlines tomorrow. I've got your back - Super Fan." Hope read Logan the message and saw him stiffen.

"We need to take your phone to Lance and see if he can trace that number," Logan told her.

"Why?" Hope was confused.

"Remember I told you someone contacted Melissa and told her they could help her?" Logan said.

"Yes." Hope nodded.

"It was Super Fan," Logan told her.

"I'll call Lance once we're done at the hospital," Hope promised Logan as they climbed out of the car and walked into the hospital. "Let's not mention this to my mom or your grandparents for now."

"Okay," Logan agreed. "But they know about the break-in."

"How much do they know?" Hope asked him.

"Not everything," Logan told her as they entered Sydney's room.

"Mommy," Sydney held out her arms for a hug and then demanded the same from Logan.

"We'll go get some coffee and something nice to eat for our princess and give you three some space," Clair said as she and Lavinia stood up.

"We'll be back soon, honey," Lavinia promised before leaving the room, pulling the door behind them.

"How are you feeling?" Logan asked Sydney.

"Much, much, better," Sydney told him. "I'm sure the doctor will let me go home tomorrow."

"You can't pretend you're feeling better so you can go home," Hope warned her.

"No, I'm feeling better," Sydney said. "I promise I'm not pretending."

"Okay," Hope gave her a silly look, making Sydney giggle.

"Mommy?" Sydney said after a brief pause in their conversation. "I want to talk to you and Logan about something."

"Okay...." Hope frowned, looking at her daughter suspiciously. "You're not going to try and get Logan to take you to Disney World, are you?"

"No!" Sydney shook her head and thought about that before smiling beguilingly at Logan. "But it's not off the table for discussion, though."

Logan laughed at the not-so-subtle hint from her. "Well, it's something we can discuss," he promised.

"Good." Sydney nodded. "But that's not what I want to talk about." She looked from Hope to Logan. "This is something else and...." She moved and pursed her lips. "I'm just going to ask." She looked at Logan and blurted out, "Are you, my father?"

EPILOGUE

Logan froze and stared at Sydney in shock, not knowing how to answer her question. His head shot up to look at Hope for direction.

"Honey," Hope cleared her throat and sat on the bed beside Sydney, putting her arm around the little girl's shoulders. "Did someone say something to you about your father?"

"No." Sydney looked at her mother. "But we are doing a family tree at school, and my teacher explained about great-grandparents, grandparents, parents, and children." She explained. "I filled your side of the family tree in and didn't know what to do with my father's side."

"Did you ask Nanna Lavinia?" Hope looked at her suspiciously.

"I did, but she said that she'd be honored to appear as my great-grandparent but to speak to you first." Sydney glanced at Logan.

He was still frozen to the spot and started to feel giddy, then realized he'd been holding his breath.

"I remember doing a project like that," was all Logan could think to say as he silently blew out a breath and had to stop himself from gasping for air.

"Okay." Hope frowned. "When was this, sweetheart, and why didn't you tell me you were doing a family tree?"

"I was going to, but then I got sick," Sydney told her. "Earlier today, Gran-gran and I started my project."

"I see." Hope's eyes narrowed.

"Don't be mad," Sydney told her, holding up her hands. "When Nanna and Gran-gran left me alone with Pops, I asked him to explain why you didn't have the same rare blood type as I did."

"Ah!" Hope smiled. "And Pops told you how it can get passed down from your father's family."

"There are only three other people in Bar Harbor, and only one in six million people have my blood group," Sydney surprised him by saying. "I Googled it."

"Where did you get a device to Google this?" Hope asked her.

"Pops!" Sydney grinned. "Do you know that there are only one-million-four-hundred people in Maine and six-million-nine-hundred people in Massachusetts? The two states where I know you've lived." She looked at her mother. "I did the math."

"You did the math?" Logan choked, thinking even his brain ached with all the stats his six-year-old daughter had just thrown at them.

"Um..." Hope raised her eyebrows and looked at Logan. "Sydney is not only musically talented." She bit her lip. "She's academically gifted, especially with math."

"I'm going to be a mathlete!" Sydney told Logan proudly before adding. "Pops told me Logan also has RH Null blood."

"Well, I guess that spoils tomorrow night's dinner conversation." Hope gave a nervous laugh. "Remember what we spoke about when I asked you if you wanted to know who your father was last year?"

"Yes." Sydney nodded. "I said I would ask you when I needed to know."

"Well, I have needed to tell you for a few weeks now," Hope told her. "I knew I couldn't keep you away from Nanna and Pops. That wouldn't be fair to you or them."

"And Logan was coming home, so it was time!" Sydney's voice dropped, and she looked up at Logan. "So you are my dad?"

Logan nodded, his voice hoarse with emotion. "Yes, I am."

"Why did you take so long to come home and find me?" Sydney's voice was barely a whisper, her eyes misted with tears.

"Because I was an idiot!" Logan ignored the pain searing through his leg and hip as he dragged a chair closer to the bed and sat in it. Leaning forward, he took her small warm hand in his. "Adults are complicated creatures. You'd think you'd have everything figured out by the time you became an adult." He swallowed as a tear rolled down her milky cheek and used his thumb to wipe it away. "Your mom and...." He looked at Hope. "We had a misunderstanding."

"Nanna said you were engaged to Melissa Shaw, the actress and pop star." Sydney frowned. "Nanna didn't like Melissa's music and that her voice was so squeaky even mice blocked their ears when she sang."

"Nanna said that?" Hope choked and looked at Sydney in disbelief.

Sydney laughed and nodded. "Nanna didn't like her much." She looked at Logan. "But I saw why when Melissa visited her one day." Her eyes widened. "I was so excited to see Melissa. I ran to greet her, and she was so rude."

"Melissa was at Nanna and Pop's house while you were there?" Hope spluttered, wide-eyed.

"Yes, three weeks ago," Sydney shocked Logan and Hope with the information. "Melissa, Nanna, and Pops had a huge argument, and Cindy took me to the cinema room to watch a Barbie movie."

"Nanna and Pops never mentioned that to me?" Hope glared at Logan.

"I didn't know about it," Logan said defensively. "I'll have a word with them."

"Have you and Mom cleared up your misunderstanding?" Sydney glanced from Logan to Hope before looking at Logan again and saying. "Do you want to be my father?"

"Of course, I do!" Logan breathed, feeling his heart jolt. "I'm so, so sorry I missed the first six years of your life, and if you'll have me, I would love to be a part of the rest of your life." He swallowed the lump in his throat. "And I promise I'll make up for missing the first part."

"You mean like a trip to Disney World?" Sydney asked hopefully.

"Nice try, little con artist." Hope sniffed, wiped her eyes, and tickled Sydney gently for her brashness.

"It was worth a try," Sydney told her before turning to Logan and smiling. "I always secretly hoped you were my father when I used to look at your pictures in Nanna and Pops's house."

"I know what you mean," Logan admitted. "I used to look at all your pictures on their walls and wonder what it would be like to be your father. Because I never stopped loving your mom."

He heard Hope's intake of breath, he looked at her, and their eyes locked. His pulse raced at the emotion he saw shining in their depths, making his stomach knot. Before they could speak again, a nurse entered the room, followed by Clair and Lavinia. Hope and Logan kissed Sydney goodnight and left the hospital.

"Do you mind if I go back with you to your place tonight and help you clean up the bakery?" Logan asked her.

"Are you sure you're up for that?" Hope asked him. "It's been quite a hectic day, and I know you're still recovering from your injuries."

Logan squashed down the surge of irritation that came when people thought he was too fragile to do things. He didn't see any pity in Hope's eyes when she'd referred to his injury, only concern for him.

"I'm fine," Logan lied. "My injuries don't even cause me that much pain and fuss these days."

Hope glanced at him as she switched on the engine and pulled out of the parking lot.

"You may be able to fool other people, Logan," Hope said softly. "But I never stopped loving you either, and because of that, I can almost feel your pain."

Logan looked at her, stunned. He'd barely heard anything beyond *I never stopped loving you.*

"Pull over!" Logan barked, frightened Hope as her head shot around to look at him wide-eyed. "Wait!" He looked at where they were and decided it wouldn't be a good idea to stop there. "Up, there's a place to pull over."

Hope's eyes were huge with worry and fright, and he felt the car speed up before careening to a stop as she pulled into the parking space.

"Are you okay?" Hope breathed frantically. "Do you need me to turn around and take you back to the hospital?"

"No! I don't need to go to the hospital, but I'm not okay." Logan undid his seatbelt, reached over, and pulled her as close to him as he could. "I need to do this."

Hope's eyes widened even more as his head lowered and his lips crushed hers. She was still for a few seconds. Hope gave a tiny mewl before her arms wound around his neck, and she moved closer to deepen the kiss.

Moments later, they came up for air and rested their foreheads together.

"I am so deeply in love with you, Hope, and I always have been," Logan's voice was gruff. "I know we have a lot to work through and bridges to rebuild." He swallowed. "Will you be interested in rebuilding them with me?"

"Yes, I would like that," Hope said softly, smiling at him. "I love you, too, Logan, and this time, I promise I won't run away again."

"And I promise I won't let you," Logan told her before crushing her lips with his again.

Once back on the road, Logan took Hope's hand in his as they made their way through Bar Harbor.

They had just pulled into the bakery parking lot when Hope got a message on her phone. Logan saw her frown as she read it before her eyes widened with shock.

"You need to see this," Hope told him. "Super Fan sent me an advanced copy of tomorrow's headlines for the Bar Harbor Daily and a few other big newspapers."

"Oh no!" Logan immediately thought the headlines were about Sydney. "I'm so sorry, Hope. I'll get my parents to help us...."

"No," Hope interrupted him. "It's not about Sydney.'

She handed him the phone, and Logan's eyes widened as he read aloud.

"Melissa Shaw's Fall from Grace, Conviction, and Pregnancy!" Logan's face fell. "She's pregnant!"

"Yes, just over six weeks, according to the article," Hope told him.

"That's why she wanted me to get engaged to her again!" Logan hissed in disbelief.

"I know she's done a lot of terrible stuff to us," Hope's voice was filled with compassion. "But I know what she must be feeling right now. It's not a great feeling to be scared and alone on top of all the hormones causing havoc with your system when you're pregnant."

They climbed out of the car, and Logan walked around to stand in front of Hope.

"You have such a big heart," Logan leaned his cane against the car and took her hands in his. "You should be America's sweetheart."

"Oh no!" Hope pulled a face. "I just want to be Bar Harbor's best caterer, event planner, and bakery."

"You are already and so much more, Hope Wright." Logan pulled her to him. "I love you," Logan whispered before his lips melded with hers in a heart-stopping kiss.

As the world faded around them while they were wrapped in each other's arms, they didn't hear Logan's cane clutter to the ground as he leaned against the car. Nor did they notice the dark figure disappear into the night after leaving a single long-stem red rose on the hood of Hope's car.

THE SECRETS IN MAINE SERIES

SECOND CHANCES DO EXIST ...

Grab your tissues and go on a journey to **Bar Harbor**, by Amy Rafferty, "The Queen Of Gorgeous Clean Mystery Romance" in the **Secrets In Maine Series.** A heart-warming mystery family saga set in a charming beach resort town in New England.

First Love in Bar Harbor (Prequel)
The Bakery in Bar Harbor (Book 1)
The Beach House in Bar Harbor (Book 2)

The Bachelor in Bar Harbor (Book 3)
The Boutique in Bar Harbor (Book 4)
The Sweet Shop in Bar Harbor (Book 5)
The Restaurant in Bar Harbor (Book 6)
The Wedding in Bar Harbor (Book 7)

Subscribe Here!

Don't miss the
Giveaways, competitions,
and 'off the press' news!

AR

Don't want to miss out on my giveaways, competitions and 'off the press' news?
Subscribe to my email list by going to https://dl.bookfunnel.com/daorxdf4jo
It is FREE!

Want to read more from

Amy Rafferty?

Love Amy Rafferty's books? If you haven't read her previous series' you are in for A REAL TREAT! All Amy's stories are

There are plenty to choose from from this talented no 1 best-selling author in kindle ebook, paperback, and in audiobook.

Head to my website to check out my books

https://www.amyraffertyauthor.com/

ABOUT THE AUTHOR

Having been described as 'The Queen Of Gorgeous Clean Mystery Romance' I am delighted that you are here. I write sweet women's romance fiction for ages 20 and upwards. I bring you heartwarming, page-turning fiction featuring unforgettable families and friends, and the ups and downs they face.

My mission is to bring you beach reads and feel-good fiction that fills your heart with emotion and love. You will find comfort in my strong female lead role models along with the men who love them. Fill your hearts with family saga, the power of friendship, second chances and later-in-life romance. I write books you cannot put down, bringing sunshine to your days and nights.

I always love to hear from you and get your feedback. Email me at books@amyraffertyauthor.com

Follow me on my socials here:

Join my 'Amy's Friends' group on Facebook - https://www.facebook.com/groups/1257329798446888/

facebook.com/amyraffertyauthor
instagram.com/amyraffertyauthor
tiktok.com/@amyraffertyauthor
amazon.com/author/amyrafferty
pinterest.com/books0171

Made in United States
North Haven, CT
12 January 2024